The Multiverse Blues

E. Chris Garrison

Other books by E. Chris Garrison

Trans Witch: College of Secrets

Alien Beer and Other Stories

Reality Check: A Tale of Quantum Entanglements

Trans-Continental: Girl in the Gears

Trans-Continental: Mississippi Queen

Blue Spirit: A Tipsy Fairy Tale

Restless Spirit: A Tipsy Fairy Tale

Mean Spirit: A Tipsy Fairy Tale

The Road Ghosts Omnibus

Contains:
Book One: Four 'til Late

Book Two: Sinking Down

Book Three: Me and the Devil

Short Story: Spectral Delivery

Dedication and Acknowledgements

*The Multiverse Blues was created during the 2020 pandemic, as a science fiction serial on my **Alien Beer Podcast**.*

Thank you to all of my listeners that followed along as I created this book, one episode at a time, airing every other week for a year. Your support meant so much to me during that difficult time.

Thanks, Mom, for being my number one fan. Knowing you were listening kept me going. I love you.

Chapter 1 – Crossroads

I suppose I could blame it all on the cat.

The chocolate brown cat zipped down the dusky alleyway ahead of me. I cursed aloud, clattering along in my ivory heels on the brick-paved street, concerned about getting alley dirt on my ivory pantsuit. I'd been led on a merry chase out of the banquet hall, down the Indianapolis city streets, and into the new, booming Arch district. I had no time for its intriguing sights, sounds, and people from other worlds right now, but I admit it'd been quite distracting.

I refused to entertain fantasies of running away through the Arch to another 'verse just now. No matter how appealing that idea might seem, I had to catch that cat!

"Come back here, that's mine!" I shouted, as though the cat could understand me.

The cat paused and looked back at me; the little white velvet box still held by its teeth. The cat's tail lashed from side to side as I approached, then it turned and leaped into a run, zipping away from me again.

I thought the cat might lose me, but then I saw it silhouetted in the crack of an open doorway, where it paused again, seeming to wait for me to catch up a bit, and then it slipped inside.

I stood just outside the open door, slightly out of breath, deciding what to do next. Should I follow? Should I go back? I glanced behind me. This side of the Arch District had a friendly sign, welcoming interdimensional travelers to "The Crossroads of America". I frowned at it, dithering while I caught my breath and worked up my nerve to trespass.

A silhouetted figure rounded the corner and called out my name. "Jules!"

Damn. My ex-boyfriend Patrick had followed me! More specifically, my *best man* Patrick followed me, huffing and puffing worse than me. I couldn't go back empty-handed. My fiancée's family didn't approve of me under the best of circumstances. If I showed up without her ring, even Sam might turn on me. If she hadn't already, for making her wait.

Hoping he didn't see, I slipped inside and shut the door behind me. It latched with a 'click'.

I found myself in a busy kitchen, full of chefs and waitstaff and food of all description. The noise and smells and movement overwhelmed my senses for a moment, but a furtive brown streak caught my eye.

Fortunately, everyone was far too busy to notice a person in white making their way to the exit, following a cat.

As I started down a long hallway, the cat disappeared around its far corner. On steadier ground now, I shucked my heels, tucked them under an arm, and ran on the cold linoleum in my ivory-stockinged feet. I followed the cat down some twists and turns into darker and darker parts of the building's service corridors. Finally, I burst through a doorway and lunged at the cat, which was now within my reach.

Except it didn't happen that way. What felt like an iron bar slammed into me, across my upper chest. My breath whooshed out of me all at once as I landed flat on my back on a hard, wooden floor. I spent a long, confused moment staring up into the rafters of a theater. As I lay there, every bad decision I'd ever made came to mind, unbidden.

And for a moment, I thought perhaps I was dying, because I heard the unearthly voice of an angel. Except the angel sang "Cross Road Blues", accompanied by a lonesome, wailing harmonica. And I smelled stale beer and possibly a hint of skunky weed.

A scarred, stubbly, grinning face eclipsed the backstage lights. "Well now, ma'am. I'm sure Miss Jasmine did something to deserve y'all bargin' in here like that. She does have a special talent for trouble. But there's no call to be grabbin' at her that way, y'hear? She's special to us in Hope's Tour, you understand."

His accent was Southern but more Gone-With-the-Wind-Southern than any real accent I'd ever heard. I tried to sit up, but he shook his head once and shoved me back to the floor. "I'm not finished, ma'am. Or is it sir?"

I caught my breath and scowled. "Neither. It's Jules. Now let me up. I need to get my ring and get back to my wedding!"

"Harlan Harper the third, at your service, I'm sure," he said, rocking back onto his haunches. "And like I said, I'm not finished. Jasmine here, well, she don't cause trouble for just the fun of it. She's usually got a reason, y'know? So she stole your ring, and I'm sure she's just as sorry as she can be about the misunderstandin', but I need you to apologize to her for scaring her like that."

"Scaring her? Look, if she hadn't taken my ring, I wouldn't have had to chase her down to get it back!"

Harlan tsked and waved a finger back and forth like an inverted pendulum. "Ah, hum. Now we could play the blame game all night, but even though you're a small person, you're a bunch bigger than our Jasmine. And thief she may be, but she deserves basic respect. Go on, now." He jutted his chin to point off to my left.

I rolled my head to see the cat, Jasmine, standing like a prim little statue, the ivory ring box at her feet. If a cat could grin, Jasmine was doing it right now, tail flicking back and forth, eyes fixed on me.

"Fine. I'm sorry for scaring you, Jasmine. Now, may I please have my ring back? I am late for my wedding. Sam's waiting for me."

The cat broke eye contact to lick her fur twice, then placed a paw on the box, as though she owned it.

Harlan stood up and offered me a hand. "Well, thank you for that. I'm glad we could be civilized about this. We'll get you back to your feller just as soon as we solve this little mystery."

I ignored his outstretched hand and stood up on my own. I dusted myself off the best I could and straightened the peplum of my suit. I ran my fingers through my blue pixie cut to push it out of my eyes. Then, I reached down to snatch my ring from Jasmine.

Harlan stopped me with a raised hand. "Aht aht. As I said, I'm sure Jasmine has a reason. Ain't that right, darlin'?"

I think all the hairs on the back of my neck stood up as the cat met his eyes and nodded.

Harlan laughed. "May want to push them eyes of yours back into your head, sir, seems they done bugged out. Jasmine's a *special* kitty. Comes from one of the 'verses where they can make animals near smart as you an' me. Smarter, maybe, since this little queen does as she pleases while we take care of her."

I took a deep breath and started to count to ten, pushing my frustration down as best I could.

But before I got to six, the stage door banged open behind me. "Jules!"

I whirled and found myself engulfed in Patrick's arms; my face smooshed into his tuxedo lapels.

Harlan's raspy laugh interrupted the somewhat one-sided embrace. "Ah, so this is your special feller, Sam?"

Patrick stepped between me and Harlan. "Not that it's your business, but *Samantha* is Jules' intended."

Harlan looked from Patrick to me, and back again, then addressed Jasmine. "Now what we gonna do about this?"

The cat folded herself into a loaf, resting her chin on the little white box.

"Hey, that's Jules' ring!" cried Patrick, coming up to speed.

I stopped him in mid-lunge, to save him from being clotheslined by Harlan. "I think this is some kind of feline hostage situation."

"Now the way I see, it," drawled Harlan, "That cat thinks you shouldn't get married today."

Patrick and I stared at Harlan. I stammered, "Wh-what are you *talking* about?"

Harlan chuckled. "Well, Jasmine always has a reason. And by takin' that there box, she's keepin' you from walkin' down the aisle. Or is she? Couldn't you just walk without the ring and get hitched anyway? Maybe you were lookin' for a way out. Maybe Jasmine here happened across you and did you a li'l favor, mister?

Patrick said, "Okay dude, we've heard enough of this crazy talk. Jules isn't a 'mister' or a 'miss'. Just get the ring from the cat and give it back to them, and we'll be out of your hair, okay?"

"Please," I said.

Jasmine let out a "mrrt!" and I looked down to see her pushing the box towards me with her nose. She trotted off watched me from behind Harlan.

"See now? That was simple," said Harlan, his grin intensifying.

I picked up the little ivory box and stared at it, my mind awhirl.

"Let's go, Jules, everyone's waiting," said Patrick, holding out a hand for me to take.

I could just picture Sam standing there at the altar, in her traditional foofy white wedding dress. Her side of the aisle full of her family and friends. Mine with co-workers from The Spyglass, the club where I tended bar for a living. A few other friends from all the various gigs I'd taken on over the years. My own family hadn't responded to the invitations. I knew what hers thought of me, but they were there for Sam, not me.

I stood at a crossroads at that moment, and I knew it. I could take Patrick's hand and go back to Samantha and her family and the life that went with all that. Or I could keep on following the cat.

A long moment passed. A new song, possibly an alien love ballad, heartbreaking in its beauty, drifted in from the stage. My resolve solidified; I knew now what I had to do.

I placed the box in Patrick's outstretched hand and closed his fingers around it. I held his gaze in mine, and said, "Tell her I love her. Tell her I'm sorry, Patrick. But I just can't."

Patrick stood there, staring at the box, breathing in and out, then he leaned over to kiss my cheek. His breath smelled of vodka.

As tears streamed down my face, Patrick unslung a backpack from behind him. My overnight bag, for after the ceremony and reception, for travel tomorrow. For the honeymoon that wouldn't happen now.

He handed my purple backpack to me, and said, "The cat's right. You're right, Jules. I knew it when you bolted, so I brought you this. I'd lay low for a while, or old man Edgewood's going to have your head on a platter for leaving his little girl standing at the altar. But it's right, Jules. It's right."

Harlan said, "When you stumbled in here, I thought Jasmine brought you here to apply for a job on the Tour. See, Hope's down a crewman since Zane left. If you're handy at all, why, you could come with us. Cat's a good judge of character, y'see."

"Where are you going?" I asked, dazed.

"Why, we're going otherwhen! Through the gates and beyond the horizon, to other universes. We're on a multiverse tour, Jules my friend!"

"I... I don't have an Arch Passport," I said. "I can't travel to another 'verse without one."

Harlan smiled. "Yeah, your world's all about control, isn't it? Zane jumped ship as soon as we got here. We still got his papers, sayin' he's from Gamma Earth. See, his wife died of cancer last year and turns out, she's still alive here in Beta. Well, her alt is. Zane told Miss Davenport, our manager, that he had to go find out whether he had a chance with her. He's not been back in the week that Hope's been playing on your Earth. I figure you could use his papers. Maybe take a little alteration, but it's no trouble. Dribbler's an expert at doctorin' papers."

I stared at Harlan. "Why would you do this for me?"

Harlan shrugged. "I'm Hope's stage manager. I could use the help. And one of the side things we do on this tour is to help folks get across the Arch to a world where they belong better. Along with moving special trade goods from one 'verse to another that wants it more."

Patrick snorted. "You're smugglers! Coyotes!"

Harlan grinned. "Heh, coyotes. Say, I like the sound of that. Call it what you will, but tight control of the Arch gates is oppressive, and if we can boost ourselves a bit by helpin' folks out, that don't seem so bad to me. So, what'll it be, Jules? You with us?"

What should I do? What else *could* I do at this point? I had a cold lump of guilt in my gut, but I said, "Sure. Wouldn't be the first roadie job I've had. I'd like to see what's out there."

Jasmine let out a happy "prrt!" Patrick sighed. Harlan clapped me on the back and smiled.

Sure, I could blame it all on the cat, but that'd be dishonest. I only have myself to blame.

Chapter 2 – Ramblin' On My Mind

"I'd better get back to the wedding," said Patrick. "You gonna be okay, chicky babe?"

I sighed at the old endearment, but touched his arm with my fingertips and said, "Yes, I think so. Maybe for the first time in years, I've got a direction. Even if I don't know where it'll lead."

"You'll keep in touch?" his eyes glinted, as though he might cry.

I nodded. "Best I can, anyway. I guess they exchange snail mail over the gates, though I'll have to ask how to address letters. Please don't tell Sam anything, okay?" I knew Patrick couldn't keep a secret, not even if his life depended on it. So, I added, "At least, give me a few days' head start."

He laughed. "Yeah, okay. I won't tell anyone where you've gone, just that I ran into you and that you..."

He left that hanging in the air between us.

I finished for him. "That I said I couldn't go through with it, and that I'm sorry."

"Think you'll be back someday?"

I nodded. "Probably. I'll take a look around and see what I can see, then maybe come back after I've made my fortune."

I stood on my tiptoes to kiss him goodbye. He flushed and stuttered a moment, then turned and left without another word.

Harlan, thankfully, had wandered a few polite feet away during this. He held a hand to his ear and spoke into a headset, giving instructions to someone else.

I waited, and soon he turned his attention to me again. "Well, don't just stand there gawping, let's see what you can do to earn your keep! Show's almost over, you can help break down and coil up cables."

I nodded, and when I didn't go anywhere, he guided me over to the edge of the stage so I could watch the end of the show.

I suppose I'd heard of Hope before. I'd seen some ads for her tour's Indianapolis dates recently on social media. I'd seen articles about the "alien singing sensation", and even a few pictures of her on stage.

None of this prepared me for seeing her in real life.

She stood in the middle of the stage, perched on a stool on a circular riser. She wore a gauzy, drapey, peach-colored gown of indistinct shape. In place of hair, she wore a similarly gauzy veil that covered the top of her head and her neck. Dozens of thin silver hoops dangled from her wrists and encircled her neck. Her skin was sleek and shiny, a light heather gray except for a paler stripe that began under her chin and widened as it traveled down to her chest. Hope's eyes were large, dark, and wide-set on her head, set back from a smooth muzzle containing pointed teeth.

From my vantage to the side and behind her, I saw what I thought was a third leg peeking out from under her gown. I soon realized the "leg" spread to wide, thin tail flukes.

Her appearance struck me as alien and strange, but rather than shocking or repulsive, I found her to be beautiful beyond describing. Her graceful movements as she sang transfixed me.

More powerful by far than her physical presence was the spell cast by her ethereal voice. She sang into a hand-held mic, and somehow, she sounded like several people singing in harmony. The trills and mournful runs she put into her singing plugged directly into my emotions. One moment, my heart soared to unimagined heights, then plummeted down, down into lonesome depths that brought more tears flowing from me. She evoked in me the feeling of being further from home than I could imagine; this reminded me, I no longer had a home myself.

"Yep, that's her magic, all right," said Harlan, whom I'd forgotten. "I'd tell you that you'll get used to it after a dozen or a hundred shows, but I'd be lying. I never have, and I've been working with Hope more years than anyone in the crew."

"She's not from around here," I said, trying to regain my cool.

"Yeah, it's not my story to tell, but Hope's from beyond the Archnet. Probably why she's got a collection of lost souls on the crew."

"Like me," I said, cold loneliness growing in my chest.

"Seems that way. Our Miss Jasmine knows how to pick 'em."

Hope wound up the sad ballad with a vocal flourish, then stood to thunderous applause. "Will there be any encores?" I asked, watching the drummer and bass guitarist stand and bow behind Hope.

"Nope, huh-uh, she never does encores. Well, rarely. Never mind that now, we gotta strike the set and get loaded up to go. Got a show in Gamma in the morning, and it's a long ways from the Arch."

The lights went down on the stage, and I followed Harlan out, feeling rather conspicuous in my white suit and heels. I shadowed him, disconnecting and coiling up audio cables and moving instruments and set pieces off the stage. The crowd stomped and cheered for more, and for a moment, I worried there might be a riot, until Hope took the mic once more, unaccompanied, and sang a sweet little goodbye song that reminded me of a lullaby. The fans cheered and accepted this as final and began filtering out the exits.

Down a short hallway from the stage was a loading dock. We loaded the equipment into the cavernous storage compartment at the rear of the largest tour bus I'd ever seen. The words *La Esperanza* were emblazoned upon the sides of the massive vehicle.

As we loaded, everyone but Hope helped out. I didn't get a chance to get names, but a smile and a nod from Harlan was all it took for the others to accept me as a part of the team.

The drummer insisted on handling his drum kit, as he packed it away in a particular way. He wore faded jeans, clumpy combat boots, and a venerable AC/DC t-shirt of a design I'd not seen before. Despite his casual attire, his hair was elegantly styled, and his subtle makeup was at least as well done as my own.

The bass guitarist wore a breathtaking deeply cut, silver-frosted, black gown being held on by the *thinnest* of spaghetti straps. She gave me a secret little wink as I helped her stow her instruments. Deeply tan, with waist-length shiny black hair, she was even shorter than me, but at least as strong.

A rather tall and sturdy woman helped with packing *La Esperanza*. She wore an orange-and-lime fluorescent pantsuit of unknown material. Her light brown hair swung at chin-length in a neat bob cut. She carried some sort of thick tablet with a keyboard on a crossbody strap, and every so often, she tapped on the keys. LED lights flashed on the device, seeming like an old '80s movie prop more than a practical modern device. Something about the way she interacted with the others fairly shouted "management", but she still did her fair share of physical labor along with the others.

Meanwhile, the cat Jasmine sat off to one side, watching us work.

As we shut the transport's hatch, Harlan asked the manager-lady, "Miz Davenport, did we get the goods packed?"

She nodded and eyed me. "All packed up and ready for Gamma. Is this the new Zane?"

Harlan invited me with a gesture to step up. "Yep, Jules here is one of Jasmine's strays."

Miz Davenport offered a hand to me, and I took it. "Marcy Davenport, tour manager."

Despite the work, her hand sat cool and firm within my own for a long moment. I said, "Jules Martin, jack of all trades, looking for a ticket off-world. And a job, if everything works out."

Her orange-painted lips quirked into the smallest of smiles. "If Jazzy thinks you're okay, that's good enough for us. Stay on as long as you like, if you always work as hard as I've seen so far."

Hope breezed past at one point but didn't stop to chat as she climbed into the passenger entrance to the giant bus.

Marcy must have noticed my expression, because she said, "Don't worry, she's always like this right after a show. I don't think she saves anything for herself. She's friendlier when you get to know her. Come on, let's rock and roll."

We all filed into *La Esperanza*, whose main cabin turned out to be a cozy living space, with two facing couches and some screens, and a kitchenette with a couple of booths with tables. A steep staircase led upwards in one corner.

Hope was not in this main area as I entered, but everyone else plopped down on the couches. I sat down next to Harlan. I deposited my purple backpack at my feet, suddenly uncomfortably aware that it now contained everything I could call my own.

"I would like a vanilla cone, love," said the bass player, her words lilting with a faint Spanish-sounding accent. Her eyes scanned me from my head to my toes and back up again. A slow, sly smile spread from her lips to light up her whole face.

The temperature of the bus went up by several degrees all at once. Maybe it was only me.

In this flustered state, I could only reply, "Huh?"

"Your ice cream suit, baby, it's delicious," she went on, fluttering her glossy-black lacquered nails as though casting a spell on me.

"Oh. This," I said, smoothing my ivory slacks. "I had, ah, more *formal* plans, but Jasmine brought me here instead. I can go change," I said, rising to my feet.

Jasmine appeared out of nowhere to curl up where I'd just been sitting. She shut her eyes and began the important business of catnapping.

"No, no, you're delightful, don't ever change," she said. "I'm Babs, by the way."

I stood there, feeling foolish. "Jules. Pleased to meet you, Babs."

Harlan clapped the drummer on the back and said, "This here's Dribbler, finest drummer, and drinker I've ever known. Stole him from Gamma's best rock band last year."

Dribbler snorted and produced a flask from somewhere. He tipped it back and offered it to me.

I accepted, then regretted it after a sip of cherry-flavored gasoline burned its way down to smolder in my stomach.

Dribbler went on. "Don't listen to Harlan. He wouldn't know good rock if it fell on his head. 'Rad Zone' ain't bad, but I got tired of Disaster Rock, wanted to diversify. Ain't much more diverse than Hope's Tour."

"Get changed if you want, might as well get comfortable," said Miz Davenport. She jutted a chin at the stairs. "Bunks are upstairs if you're shy. Yours'll be the vacant one, last one on the left."

As I ascended the stairs, the bus began a low humming, which I took to be engines, though they didn't sound like diesel to me. Electric, maybe?

Like a low-ceilinged train sleeper car, I found the upstairs a bit more cramped. Several doors lined the narrow hallway on either side. Curtains hid the furthest forward compartment. I peeked behind the curtains, expecting a dressing room, but instead found a forward observation lounge. It could seat four people if they were *very* friendly. The heavily tinted windows revealed the lights of Indianapolis as the bus wound its way around the city streets, towards the Arch Authority.

I also found Hope, draped across one of the couches, wearing some kind of scuba-like coverall. Her hands turned out to be mittens, her feet toeless splayed pads. Her tail curled around her and her flukes flipped idly. She radiated elegance, even in her exhausted pose.

Her eyes caught mine, and she drew in a sharp breath.

"Oh, I'm sorry!" I cried. "I didn't mean to intrude."

She shook her head "No, *La Esperanza* is for all of us, not just me." She made music even with her speaking voice, her words sung with a beautiful trill. "I... just need time alone after a show."

I nodded. "I'll just change out here, don't mind me," I said.

Hope favored me with a beautiful, shy, alien smile. "Welcome to my crew, Jules. May we each find the best of all possible worlds."

I had no idea what to say to that cryptic greeting, so I just smiled and withdrew. There turned out to be a small, but serviceable bathroom with a shower. I took advantage of these facilities with indulgent gratitude. Once I'd dried off, I slipped into a baggy green sweater tunic and black leggings with silver Converse sneakers. I thanked my earlier foresight to pack a carry-on for the overnight; I had a couple more outfits inside my backpack, along with a couple of weeks' worth of other necessities.

I tossed my backpack and ice cream suit and heels into the bunk Miz Davenport had indicated. It still said "Zane" on the door.

I descended the stairs and was greeted by applause from the others, much to my surprise.

I stopped and blinked at them.

"Congratulations, baby, you passed the first test," purred Babs. "If you can shower while the bus is moving, that says a lot about you."

Miz Davenport added, "That, and you've got better hygiene than most of the crew."

"Hey!" protested Dribbler, when Marcy's eyes fell on him. "I'm just all about conserving water, that's all."

The bus came to a stop, and a voice like someone gargling a hive of bees spoke over the bus's intercom. "The Transportation and Security Administration requests that all sentient beings disembark for processing, and so that they may search our vehicle."

As one, the crew groaned.

Harlan told me, "Sometimes, they give us a pass since Hope's a big deal an' all. Not this time."

A cold lump formed in my stomach. "Uh, I still don't have a passport."

Dribbler stood and handed me his flask again. "Relax, pigeon! It'll be fine. Let ol' Dribbler handle things for ya!"

Babs hid a smile behind her hand.

Dribbler called to the ceiling, "Zamboni, please fetch me some glow juice, okay?"

The buzzing electronic voice replied over the intercom, "It will be done."

I squinted at Dribbler. "Uh, Zamboni?"

Dribbler shrugged. "It's a nickname. He makes things smoother."

"But who is--"

A panel opened from the front of the bus, and a science fiction horror crawled out.

Okay, that's very human-centric of me, I know. But having never seen real, live robotics more advanced than the Boston Dynamics robot dogs, Zamboni gave me the willies.

The robot consisted of a glassy globe atop a central cylinder the size of two stacked beer kegs, with three legs and three arms. The spindly appendages all ended in three-digited claws. The head-globe revealed no specific face but seemed to contain an irregularly faceted crystalline mass of some kind.

Zamboni scrambled past me and up a wall and onto the ceiling like a deranged metal Spider-Man. The robot opened a hatch on the ceiling and reached inside, rummaging around.

"Zamboni," said Dribbler, with a gesture towards the robot clinging to the ceiling.

I was far too busy gawping to come up with an intelligent reply.

The others began moving around the cabin. Babs climbed the stairs and disappeared from view.

Harlan put a hand on my shoulder as he moved past me towards the back of the bus. "Don't worry your pretty little head none about Zamboni. He's tame as my grandma's sheepdog. About as smart, too. I mean, sure, Zamboni knows a lot more words, but a dog gets what you *mean* better, if you follow."

I nodded, watching Zamboni clamber back down to the floor. Dribbler fished a shot glass out of a panel above the seats and held it out. Zamboni unscrewed the thermos and poured an ounce of greenish-yellow liquid into it, then set about returning the thermos where it came from.

Dribbler held the shot glass out to me. "Drink up!"

I took the shot glass and examined it. Printed on the side was the likeness of an octogenarian Elvis head, with the words, "Graceland 2000". The liquid sat heavy in the shot glass, and it gave off the aroma of lemon-scented furniture polish.

I peered at Dribbler over the rim. "Yeah, uh, is now really the time for a shot?"

Dribbler grinned. "Trust me. This is your passport to Gamma Earth. It's slightly radioactive."

"Radioactive! Are you kidding?"

Marcy hustled past, carrying a stack of folders and loose papers. "Oh, don't be such a big baby. Drink it if you want to come with us."

Doubts rose like ghosts within me. "Why? Is this some kind of hazing?"

Dribbler rolled his eyes. "What do you know about Gamma Earth?"

I thought back to what I'd seen on the web, and said, "It's like here, except they had a war in the Sixties. Cities got nuked. Took forever to work back up to where they were before the war."

Dribbler nodded. "And everyone from Gamma Earth has radioactive isotopes in their systems. Like me."

"You're from Gamma? Okay, but is this safe for Beta people like me?"

Dribbler frowned. "Dude. I know we only just met but give me a *little* credit. I'm not out to poison ya. Give me a little leap of faith, and we'll get ya through this, okay?"

Already far outside my comfort zone, I thought about why I *should* trust Dribbler, or anyone here.

"Mrow!" Jasmine the cat sat up and stared at me and jutted her chin like a person tossing back a shot.

I guess the cat was as good a reason to trust these people as any. Jasmine's comfort spoke volumes about the relative kindness of Hope's crew.

"Okay, Jasmine, if you say so," I said, then I tossed back the radioactive liquid. That it tasted like thick, flat Mountain Dew comforted me not at all.

Hope descended the stairs, and she sang, "Must we do this?"

Miz Davenport took one of Hope's mitten-hands in her own. "I'm sorry to say we do. This place is almost as bad as Achse."

"And getting worse, if you ask me," said Babs, following Hope. "We all have our papers?"

Everyone nodded in turn, then Miz Davenport handed me a folder. "Here are Zane's. I took the liberty of substituting a picture of you. I wasn't sure about some of the details, but this is just to get through."

"You'll be fine," said Harlan.

"You keep saying that, but you don't know the TSA of my world like I do," I said, glancing at the papers inside. "Zane Dawson? Am I supposed to be some kind of soap opera star?"

Dribbler snorted. "Yeah, yeah. We don't have those back on Gamma. But we do have rock-n-roll, so that name'll do."

At a knock on the door, Miz Davenport glanced at each one of us, then opened it outward. She stepped out and spluttered indignation on our behalf, but the uniformed TSA agents remained impassive, taking the stack of folders and papers from her.

One by one, we filed out to be processed. Zamboni got a thorough going-over but was sent back before anyone else. Dribbler told me they considered him "equipment", so there was less paperwork to do.

A couple of agents followed Zamboni inside *La Esperanza*. I wondered if they'd harass poor Jasmine.

Miz Davenport walked through the millimeter-wave body scanner and answered some questions with undisguised irritation. She hovered around, fussing over each of the inspections, once her own was completed.

Babs charmed her way through hers, making risqué jokes as they passed wands all around her body. Had it been me in her place, I'd have been upset at the extra attention the agents gave to searching her.

Dribbler plunked his boots into a tray and gave a warning to the agents. They laughed, then shot him a dirty look as the boots passed by them. As he passed through the scanner, lights around the machine flashed blue. I gathered this meant they picked up on his background radiation. After a thorough wanding and searching, they passed Dribbler through.

Harlan breezed through without any trouble.

My turn. My mouth dried out as I handed my papers to the agent.

She looked from the papers to me and back. "Zane Dawson? Ain't I heard of you somewhere?"

I faked a smile. "I certainly hope so," I said, nodding at the bus.

She fixed me with a glare. "That supposed to be funny?"

"No. I mean, yes, it's just that we're on tour, and--"

"Yeah, yeah. I gotta say, you don't look like a Zane to me."

I drew a breath, paused, then said, "What do I look like, then?"

She shrugged and went back to the papers. "A Jane, maybe. Can't tell for sure. But it's none of my business what people choose to do in their own bedrooms."

I let this comment pass by me as though I hadn't heard it.

She waved me through the scanner.

I stepped inside. The scanner passed down and up again. The blue radioactivity lights flashed, then turned red. I heard bolts slam shut as an alarm squealed.

The scanner locked me in!

"Hey!" I cried, my voice far too loud in my own ears because of the cramped, closed plexiglass booth.

A speaker crackled next to my ear. "We're showing an anomaly."

I hated this part. The agents had only two buttons, trouser guy and skirt lady. Neither applied for me.

"I'm non-binary," I explained.

"Yeah, we get that. Yeah, no, different anomaly. Your face scan doesn't match Zane Dawson's entry records two weeks ago."

I sighed, hopes sinking. Now I might get away from it all by going to TSA jail. Federal prison, maybe? I bluffed. "I was a bit hung over when I got here. Bags under my eyes. Dehydrated. Maybe that's the difference?"

The agent who'd interrogated me shook her head. "Naw, this is something else, sunshine. Or should I say, Jules Martin?"

I slumped. It was over. Dribbler's plan had failed, and now my troubles multiplied far beyond just skipping my own wedding.

A strange keening trilled outside, penetrating even the thick walls of the booth. It warbled and modulated into a sort of music. Alien music.

I turned to peer back at Hope, whose mouth yawned open as she sang. Her eyes closed; she fluttered her hands as though she might float up into the air through the power of song alone.

The TSA agents all turned and stared at her, eyes widening, mouths hanging open. Their faces softened into something I thought I'd never see.

The TSA agents *smiled*.

A timeless moment elapsed as she sang, and then she shut her mouth and let her arms hang down at her sides. Her eyes opened and fixed upon me. She winked.

The bolts shot back, and the booth opened to let me out. The fresh air of the Arch station flooded in, and I stepped out and retrieved my sneakers and cell phone. I eyed my agent, and she shrugged. "You know, it happens. The machine had you mistaken for someone else. But you're radioactive like anyone from Gamma, so Jules is just your local twin here. You're free to go, Zane Dawson."

I just carried my shoes as I walked away, not wanting to be there any longer than I had to be.

"Funny thing, *Zane*," she called after me. "You're the second 'twin' in our system this week. System says another one of you arrived last Wednesday."

I let out a nervous laugh. "If you see me again, say hi for me, will you?"

"Will do!"

I watched them wave Hope through without even scanning her, since their equipment had no way to deal with her physiology. And, I think because she'd charmed them with her singing.

Once we'd all passed inspection, we got back onto the bus and took seats.

"That was closer than I'd have liked," I said to Dribbler. "I thought I was done there for a horrible moment."

Dribbler shrugged. "It is what it is, dude. Now, we're on our way through the Arch! First time for you, right?"

I nodded.

He grinned. "Why don't you slide on up front with Zamboni and watch the show?"

The others nodded agreement.

"I think it's damned disturbing," said Harlan, "But worth seeing at least once."

I made my way up to the front and let myself into the driver's compartment. Zamboni perched on a bucket seat in front of the steering wheel, using all three arms and one of his legs to work controls.

"Uh hi," I stammered, "I'm Jules."

The robot made no sign he heard me.

"Hello, Zamboni?"

"Greetings," he said.

I attempted to make conversation. "What are you doing, Zamboni?"

"I am driving. I am sealing internal systems for traversal. I am speaking to Jules Martin. Please sit."

I sat in the other bucket seat and swiveled to look forward.

The Arch stood before us. A two-story semicircle, its perfect mirror surface reflected the front of *La Esperanza* back at us. For all the world, we seemed to be in the middle of a low-speed game of chicken with ourselves.

Everything I'd read about passing through an Arch to another universe had mentioned the chance for motion-sickness, and that it could have psychedelic effects on people. Seemed all reports said that there's nothing you can do to prepare for the experience.

I'd also heard it said that time didn't work right in between one Arch and another; time spent between didn't happen in the worlds on either side of the passage.

"How long will traversal take?"

The robot didn't answer me.

Feeling a little irritated, I repeated, "*Zamboni*, how long will traversal take?"

"Traversal is instantaneous. Passengers will experience approximately sixty-seven minutes elapsed time between Arches."

Before I could ask any more nervous questions, the bus seemed to smoosh into its reflection. I can't recall what happened when my face pushed through my own reflection, because I passed out at that point.

I sat at a table with a checkered tablecloth. Sitting in front of me on a plate was a stack of blue pancakes. The stack stretched upwards into the starry sky, thinning to a line, then a thread, then beyond my ability to see. Each pancake looked like a flattened Earth.

Zamboni danced around the table. The robot poured glowing green-and-yellow syrup from a thermos down the side of the pancakes.

Babs lay across the table, her head propped up by one hand. She wore Jasmine's face instead of her own. She licked her nose and laughed at me.

Sam and Patrick stuck their heads out from inside the stack of pancakes. Sam burst into tears and threw her bouquet at me, and I had to duck out of the way. Patrick gave me a thumbs-up, but then he too burst into tears.

Curtains pulled aside, and Hope and Dribbler began to play "Come on Into My Kitchen" and the pancakes fell into a pile. They spilled off the table, Sam and Patrick lost among the myriad Earth cakes and sticky syrup.

The floor began to fill with the Earths, and I had to swim to stay on top of them, my arms and legs slowed by the sticky radioactive syrup.

At one point, I was dragged under by unseen hands, but I kicked my way to the top again, only to find myself face-to-face with another me.

We both gasped, then their eyes narrowed, and they put their hands-on top of my head and shoved me back under the deepening pile of pancakes.

I fought for breath and breathed in syrup and crumbs.

I coughed and fought and lost all sense of direction.

I screamed!

My eyes flew open, and I found myself laid out on one of the long couches of the main cabin of *La Esperanza*.

Miz Davenport leaned over me. "Welcome back. Have any interesting dreams, hon?"

I nodded. "I'd rather not talk about it."

She smiled and patted my cheek. "I don't blame you. I only did that one time myself. Still messes with me even back here."

I sat up in my seat, head swimming a little. "What did that TSA agent mean when she said someone with my face had been through there last week?"

Harlan answered, "I reckon one of your alts passed by, into your world, from Gamma."

"So, there's another one of me floating around my world?"

Miz Davenport and Harlan nodded.

"Does that happen often? Running into yourself?"

Harlan shrugged. "Never have run into another one of me, but I know Dribbler has."

Dribbler groaned. "Yeah, I don't recommend it."

"Why not?" I asked.

"Well, you know how most people don't like hearing their own voice on a recording?"

"Yeah?"

"Well, it's like that but a hundred times worse, when you see them do every creepy little thing you didn't know you do. Not sure it makes sense, but it just feels wrong. Even worse when they do something you *wouldn't* do. Kinda like expecting another step downstairs when you're already at the bottom."

I didn't really follow, but I had another question. "So, what's my twin doing on Beta then?"

He shrugged. "Maybe looking for you. Maybe looking for the Beta version of someone else in their world? Maybe just getting away from it all, like you?"

I pictured this other Jules running into Sam and Patrick. Maybe posing as me. A heavy feeling weighed in my gut. "Well, I guess I hope they have better luck with my life than I did."

Chapter 4 – Last Fair Deal Gone Down

Interdimensional travel is kind of boring. Well, most of it was, during the part we spent between the Arch on my own Beta Earth, and the one on Dribbler's Gamma Earth.

Once the hallucinations and weird dreams had passed, it was just a bus ride, more or less. The crew sat and chatted about the last show, and there was some talk of payment and goods, but my head still needed some recovery time, so I zoned out. Jasmine curled up next to me on the couch and joined me in ignoring the conversation.

A few minutes later, my curiosity got the better of me, and I rejoined Zamboni in the driver's compartment. Knowing the robot's lack of social skills, I decided to just watch out the windows with him in silence.

The outside consisted of an amorphous, multi-colored murk. I thought of it as technicolor fog. At times, tendrils of mist came at us with a disturbing solidity, but Zamboni seemed unconcerned. Not that I could read any expressions on his crystalline face. Or even make out a face, for that matter.

The shifting shapes of the fog reminded me of watching the undulations of a lava lamp; shapes emerged and morphed and retreated. Sometimes the shapes resembled distorted faces, other times blobby animals seemed to stretch out of other masses like taffy, only to squish into other, unrecognizable shapes.

Once, for only a second, the fog cleared, and I caught a glimpse of an actual *place*. I saw a grassy field, full of bison. A frozen column of black smoke loomed over one horizon. There was much more detail, but like a dream, I only retained so much from that flicker of a moment.

After a little more time watching the space between worlds, outside of time, my stomach began to churn with a sort of motion sickness. On my way back to the main cabin, I patted Zamboni on his cylindrical casing, grateful that I didn't have his job. The robot remained impassive.

As I returned, Miz Davenport said with a smile, "Did you see any slithy toves?"

I snorted. "I don't think so. Not unless they resemble buffalo?"

She tapped her lips, considering this. "Not usually. They tend to gyre and wabe, like the Jabberwock. Why, did you see some buffalo outside?"

I nodded. "I think so. Just a flash of a place in the fog, but it was gone as soon as it came."

Harlan slapped the couch cushion next to him to invite me to sit. "Good thing we didn't bump into any. Next time, you should try to mark the time and position, it might be worth something to the Arch Authority. They give bounties to folk who find new worlds to check out."

Dribbler added, "It's a bit like tuning an analog radio. Sometimes, if you're watching very carefully, you can 'tune in' on a 'verse. If it's still there when the Arch Authority sends someone to check it out, they might be able to send explorers through."

"Pay's pretty good, even if it's really rare," said Babs. "But only if it works out, and only if it's useful. Empty worlds are good for resources, but ones with people we can talk to and trade with are worth a lot more."

Babs' last word dragged out like a singer holding a note, "mooooooooore."

During that elongated several seconds, the room distorted; it stretched out and snapped back, and dizziness threatened to overwhelm me.

At the end of Babs' elongated word, my head reattached itself to my body, I found Harlan had laid a steadying hand on my upper arm.

"Not as bad as your first time, hmm?" he said.

I patted his hand with my own, and he withdrew. I smiled and nodded. "Yes, I didn't hallucinate or pass out, so that's progress anyway."

Zamboni's voice buzzed over the intercom. "Gamma Earth Arch Authority welcomes us to the world. Current programming is to continue to the scheduled cargo rendezvous, and then on to the first musical engagement."

Babs grinned at me and said, "Want a glimpse of your first new world, *chica*?"

I nodded.

She touched a pad near the windows on her side of the bus. The windows shifted from dark opaque to merely tinted.

The terminal outside the Gamma-side Arch was gray, gravelly, and dusty. Other large vehicles and shipping containers lined the roadway leading from the Arch. People in coveralls milled around, carrying tools or clipboards. Flickering fluorescent lights covered the ceiling of the terminal, illuminating everything in a dim bluish glow.

"Not much to see, is there?" I said, a bit disappointed.

Babs laughed. "Wait 'til we get to Delta. *That* is something to see, let me tell you! Gamma's got plenty of more interesting sights than this grungy warehouse. It's gorgeous at twilight times. People dress pretty here too. Classy."

I saw what she meant. Once we passed out of the cargo area of the terminal, I noticed people lining up to board other buses and trams. At first glance, I felt like I'd fallen into an old movie. Men wore fedoras and sharply tailored suits. Women sported flouncy knee-length dresses, as well as hairdos piled high upon their heads. As I looked closer, I noticed that everyone wore masks. Men's masks tended to be plain white, while women often had masks in colors and patterns to match their clothing.

I confess I felt a bit disappointed not to see anyone like me, only men and women, with no room for anything in-between.

Perhaps they all dressed in formalwear for travel? I hoped casualwear would allow lines to be blurred a bit more, or I'd very likely stand out like an alien in this place.

After *La Esperanza* drove out from under the great canopy of the terminal area, I could scarcely see anything outside. The late evening of my world had already gone dark in Gamma. Lights shone from windows in buildings all around the Arch terminal, and the few vehicles on the streets. I wondered if maybe time on the other side of the gates might be different, or if perhaps I'd emerged in a different part of the world.

"Is this still Indianapolis, but Gamma-style?" I asked Dribbler.

He nodded. "Yeah. Arches don't always line up, but they do between Beta and Gamma. Naptown's pretty different here; it wasn't one of the cities hit in the war, being so far inland, and not a strategic target. Grew a lot after, though, but it's still a fraction the size of your Indy. Not as many people around and the nukes scared people away from city living."

The thought gave me a chill, so I changed the subject. "How far to the rendezvous?"

Miz Davenport answered, "Not far, it's out by the airport. A warehouse. Dribbler, we'll need your services as a local guide again."

Dribbler's face fell, and he stared at his shoes. "Aw, Marcy. You know how I feel about this place. I left here for a reason."

She nodded and pressed her lips together. She paused to tuck a lock of her hair behind an ear before replying, "All the same, we can't afford to get swindled again. *You* know the people here. Please, James?"

He glanced up at her and sighed. "Okay, but I'm not goin' alone. I'd like to take Babs and Jules with me?"

Babs gave him a little salute and a wink. "Ab-so-*lutely*, darlin'! I won't let them bully you, sweetie."

Dribbler looked at me with puppy eyes, and I wondered what this world had done to him.

I said, "Won't I, um, kinda stand out?"

Harlan coughed. "Yeah, I figure that's the idea. By comparison, Dribbler'll fit *right* in."

An icy twist in my gut must have shown on my face because Harlan held up both hands, palms out. "Whoa there, doll. I don't mean you no harm. You're pretty as a picture, but these folks are a bit more, ah, *traditional*, if you catch my meaning. They skipped a couple of your world's social revolutions while they clawed their way back from the stone age."

As Harlan spoke, something haunted flickered behind Dribbler's eyes.

"Well, okay, if you think I can help, I'll go with you," I said, feeling a little protective of the big drummer for some reason.

Babs switched sides of the bus to squish herself between me and Harlan, putting a slender arm around my shoulders. She guided my chin with her fingertips so that I would see her dark, wide eyes looking into mine. "Honey baby, you'll be fine. You just remember you're a badass, okay? Their ways aren't like yours. They won't know what to make of you, and that's a good thing. We want them off balance, you understand?"

I took in a deep breath, and let out some hot, jagged feelings with a slow exhale. "Yeah, I guess so."

Dribbler chimed in, "Believe me, dude, they'll know you're from another 'verse. Me, well, let's say having someone local diverge from customs doesn't set well with them. At all."

I decided not to take the bait by asking how Dribbler might be divergent. I changed the subject again. "What do you even use for money between worlds?"

Miz Davenport answered. "Barter, mostly. Precious metals and gems, sometimes. We'll even take local currency if it's a place we're planning on coming back to, or if they have an exchange set up with a friendly neighboring 'verse. This time, it's a bit of a *cultural* exchange."

"What kind of culture?" I asked.

Babs giggled. "Ever heard of The Beatles?"

I snorted. "Duh?"

She grinned and patted my cheek. "Beta hasn't. Not The Doors, either."

Dribbler protested. "But we *do* have Elvis. He doesn't tour anymore, but he's still the King."

Babs rolled her eyes. "Sure. But the point is, we got what they didn't have, and vice versa. We're trading them a stack of CDs and some nice digital-to-analog recording equipment. For that, they're giving us a couple of crates of vinyl records that'll be a hit in Delta. That, and some other stuff."

I'd heard some bootleg recordings from other 'verses, and I could see the appeal. The MPAA and RIAA of my world came down *hard* on anyone caught distributing interdimensional recordings. This helped traveling musicians like Hope's Tour, however, since it was one of the only ways Beta folks could get a legal sample of the music of other worlds.

Maybe a half-hour later, we pulled off the main road into a dark maze of warehouses. The area wasn't nearly as well-lit as I would have liked.

Miz Davenport approached me, and said, "Just in case," as she handed me what I took for a garage door opener at first. Then I noticed two shiny metal prongs and a safety switch along with the big concave button.

She said, "It's a taser, from Alpha. Try not to use it unless you need to, okay?"

I nodded and clipped it inside my sweater's sleeve.

Harlan opened a hatch in the floor, towards the back, and he and Miz Davenport lifted out a few rugged plastic crates and put them on a wheeled cart. The door opened double-wide this time, and a ramp descended along with the stairs I'd already seen. Floodlights from either side of the hatch illuminated the near-empty parking lot.

Cold air rushed into the cabin, and I shivered despite my sweater and leggings. The air of Gamma smelled wintrier than the autumn air back home had. That, and it had a bit of a plasticky, metallic, campfire quality to it. Jasmine bounded down the stairs and sniffed at the night air and lashed her tail back and forth.

"Shouldn't we wear masks or something?" I said as I spied a quartet of men in suits and masks standing protectively around a small pallet of wooden crates.

Dribbler shrugged. "Maybe later. A few minutes won't hurt ya any. Besides, they're more for fashion than anything these days."

I helped Dribbler and Babs roll the cart of goods down the ramp. It was a fair bit heavier than I expected.

Jasmine bounded up onto the cart, sitting in a most regal fashion as we rolled her out into the parking lot. I smiled at her, but she only had eyes for the four masked men. Her tail jerked and lashed, and I could feel the cat's agitation.

"Hey, what's up with the kitty?" I asked Babs.

Babs glanced at Jasmine, then frown lines creased her forehead. She turned to look behind us, and murmured, "Not sure, but look sharp, *chica*."

When we were a few yards from the pallet of crates, Babs and I stopped, while Dribbler swaggered up to meet the others. "Dudes. Is one of you 'Smiley'?"

A rail-thin guy in a maroon suit and hat stepped forward to meet Dribbler. The man's eyebrows hovered above his steel-gray eyes like a pair of salt-and-pepper wooly worms. He offered a hand to Dribbler. "Mister MacGowan. So nice of you to flutter by," he said, to the titillation of the other three.

In my peripheral vision, I noticed Babs tense and straighten, her hands hanging free by her sides. Jasmine leaped down from our cart and slipped off into the shadows.

Dribbler hesitated, then shook the man's hand. "Ah, yeah. So, are we doing business, bud?" His voice dropped to a soft growl. "Or maybe you came here to sing some old show tunes with me?"

The three guys with Smiley took a step toward Dribbler. Babs slid up behind her bandmate to back him up. I interposed myself between the cart and Smiley's men. My heart beat faster and my breath quickened. I had no idea what I'd do if this turned into a fight, but I palmed the taser and slipped off the safety. Just in case.

Smiley spread his hands, palms up, and his men stopped where they were. "You're a very *funny* man, Mister MacGowan! But I don't care who you're *funny* with," he said, eyeing me a long moment. "I'm just joking with you. Let's trade, 'kay?"

The tension in the air relaxed just a bit.

Jasmine appeared on top of the wooden crates, sniffing and pawing at the edges. I watched her leap to another crate to sniff it too. Her mouth hung open just a little as she let out a low moaning growl. She met my gaze and shook her head twice, from side to side, then jumped down.

"Babs," I said, just loud enough for her to hear. "Jasmine's not happy about the cargo."

With a flick of her hand behind her back, Babs acknowledged what I'd said, and I took her warning to be wary.

My gut said I needed to do something more direct. I stepped up to the crate and said, "You don't mind if we take inventory, do you, Smiley?"

Smiley laughed. "What, you don't trust me, cream puff?" He turned his gaze back to Dribbler, and said, "Your little friend don't trust me, *dude*. What are we gonna do about that?"

Dribbler's expression clouded, and he said, "If we want to inspect the merchandise, I think you should let us. Standard business practice. You understand, don't you Smiley?"

A guy in a houndstooth suit moved in and touched my waist, to guide me to a different crate. I elbowed him in the ribs, then worked at the fastening on the crate Jasmine had indicated.

"Boss!" warned a guy in a charcoal suit, taking a few quick steps to the side.

The remaining masked man took several steps backward and drew a pistol, which he aimed at my head.

I ducked down to hide from him behind the crate. Rough hands grabbed my shoulders and I cried out. Then, I jabbed the taser into the guy's thigh and squeezed the button.

ZZZAAP.

The rather satisfying electric jolt knocked Mr. Houndstooth into a convulsing heap on the pavement next to me.

CRACK!

A gunshot rang out from behind me, and Smiley and the other two ran in different directions, away from the crates.

Harlan's voice bellowed "Jules! Get away from there!"

I scrambled to my feet and dashed back towards the ramp.

Smiley called out an unintelligible order to one of his men.

CRACK!

BOOM!

A wave of heat raced a thunderclap, which flung me onto the ramp. I landed in a tangle with Babs, who'd gotten there first. I looked up to see Harlan standing in the doorway, a long rifle in his hands, aimed at the sky. Jasmine stood at his side, her fur fully poofed, eyes round and wild.

I peered back over my shoulder to look for Dribbler, but only saw a towering, fiery mushroom where the wooden crates had been.

Chapter 5 – I Believe I'll Dust My Broom

"Dribbler!" I cried as I struggled to my feet. I scanned the lot, squinting through clouds of dust and debris kicked up by the explosion. My new friend was nowhere I could see. As the fiery mushroom burnt out, I could see even less in the dimmer light.

Babs darted off back the way we'd come; the dust and dark swallowed her whole. Jasmine the cat bounded after her.

"Hush!" hissed Harlan, leaping from the ramp to the ground beside me. "Get down or move. You're a sittin' duck, and givin' away your position with your damn fool shouting. Gonna get you killed. Maybe me with you."

I was about to argue with him, but I was cut off by a shot out in the darkness. I threw myself to one side, away from Harlan and the ramp. I stayed close to the tour bus until I reached its rear end, away from *La Esperanza*'s floodlights, but still in the bus's shadow from the parking lot's orange sodium lights. A gust of wind pushed a wall of dust and smoke away from me, and I spied a crumpled figure on the pavement about fifteen feet away from me.

I'd need to venture out into the open, but if it might be Dribbler, I'd have to take that chance.

Hunched low, I crept out into the lot step by step toward the body. Every nerve in my body sang out an alarm, knowing that I made a fine target to anyone outside of the dust cloud. My heart thundered in my ears and my eyes stung with tears from more than airborne grit. All the while, I struggled to reign in my rasping breaths.

Despite all that, I almost let out a yelp of joy as I realized that not only was the form on the ground my new friend Dribbler, but his chest rose and fell as I reached him.

I patted his face and whispered his name in his ear. "Dribbler, are you okay? Wake up, we have to get you out of here!" His skin was clammy to my touch, his face pale and wan.

Dribbler groaned and coughed, but his eyes remained shut. I pulled open both eyes and saw that his pupils were dilated but unseeing.

I had a terrible dilemma. Since Dribbler was likely in shock, I knew I shouldn't try to move him. But if I left him here, he could get shot, or he could get worse without better care than I could give him.

Another gunshot ripped the air not far away from me, lighting up the smoke with its flash.

That decided me. I hooked my hands under Dribbler's armpits and dragged him back toward the ramp. Halfway there, he groaned and convulsed and vomited. I had to stop to turn him onto his side and cleared his airway with my fingers.

As I tended to Dribbler, running feet skittered gravel as someone smallish rushed past me. Some meaty thuds from somewhere in the dark told the story of a fistfight, followed by the scrabbling of feet and the sound of another body hitting the ground.

I redoubled my efforts to move Dribbler. We made it nearly to the edge of the cone of brilliance cast by the bus's entry floodlights when Jasmine leaped into my path and hissed. I stopped more out of reflex than anything. Jasmine and I just stared at each other, each breathing hard, for a long moment. She shook her head, then turned to look back behind her towards where I'd last seen Harlan.

After a few heartbeats, I felt the need to move forward, but Jasmine kept blocking my path, warning me back with a low growl.

I pleaded with her. "Jasmine, Dribbler's hurt, I have to get him to the bus and get him medical attention!"

The cat shook her head once more, and then the floodlights went out, plunging us into near darkness.

Jasmine disappeared, leaving me free to continue dragging the big guy.

When I reached the ramp, Marcy ducked out from underneath it and helped me pull Dribbler inside.

In the now dark interior of *La Esperanza*, I said, "I think he's in shock. Does anyone know more than just first aid?"

Marcy's whisper came from close to my ear. "Hope does. She has medical devices. Alien technology. They can help heal him. I hope."

Just then, footsteps clattered on the stairs and Babs fell to the floor next to me, gasping for breath.

"Are you—" I began.

More shots barked outside, and a couple pinged off the bus's hull. Jasmine leaped into the cabin, followed by Harlan, who landed heavily. He called out, "Zamboni, lock us down and get us out of here!"

Zamboni replied over the intercom, "I will comply."

The hatch pulled shut and the engine whined and I had to grab onto Dribbler to keep him from sliding around the cabin as the bus swung in a series of tight arcs.

Light from outside slanted crazily as we passed streetlamps at high speed. I heard another ping of a shot ricocheting off of *La Esperanza*'s skin, then all fell quiet.

Hope appeared by my side, holding a frisbee-shaped device. The device's underside lit Dribbler's pasty face with a warm yellow glow. Dribbler took in a deep breath and let it out in a gust, and some color returned to his cheeks.

The bus's interior lights flickered to life and I found myself and Dribbler in a circle of faces. The whole crew seemed to hold their breath, watching Hope work.

I turned to look at Hope as she worked. I had more or less decided on my own that she and her people were descended from porpoises or other cetaceans. Her glossy smooth grey skin shone in the dim interior lights; her enigmatic black eyes focused on Dribbler. She wore a filmy green gown that appeared to be damp like it was fresh out of the washing machine. As I sat within a foot of her, I couldn't help but notice the alien beauty of this creature. This *person*, I corrected myself.

Hope glanced over at me, and my face burned with embarrassment. *She'd caught me staring!* She favored me with a smile filled with little pointed teeth, and then returned to her work. Her tail swished behind her and brushed my ankle, and somehow that made me feel a little better.

Harlan broke the silence. "Get any of 'em?"

Babs replied, "Think so! Winged 'im at least."

I looked up and around the cabin at the crew and asked, "What was that all about anyway? Were they trying to kill Dribbler?"

Babs and Harlan exchanged a look, then Babs answered, "Maybe. But they wanted us to bring that Trojan-horse bomb on board. I think they were trying to kill us all, *chica*."

"Fuckers," whispered Dribbler, his eyes open a slit. "I shoulda known better than to deal with Smiley."

Miz Davenport crossed her arms. "You didn't know. Your contact told you-"

"My contact," growled Dribbler, "set us up." He tried to rise, but Hope pushed him back to the floor with a gentle three-fingered mitten hand.

Hope hummed a soothing tune and sang to Dribbler, "You will be okay, my dear. But you will need to rest."

Dribbler's eyes fluttered, then his face went slack as he fell asleep.

Hope glanced at Marcy Davenport and Babs, and then at the couches, and the two human women nodded and picked the big guy up and laid him there. Jasmine slinked her way from the back of the couches onto Dribbler's chest, where she curled up and joined him in a cat nap.

"Thanks for the warning, Jasmine," I said to the cat.

Jasmine's ears pivoted towards me, and her tail flicked acknowledgment.

Hope stood and sang to the rest of us, "Sleep is healing, sleep is good. We all need to get some, and St. Louis is hours away yet. Rest well, my crew."

Before I could ask more about the bomb and the attempt on our lives, the crew followed Hope's suggestion and headed to quarters. Hope remained by Dribbler's side. Though I was sorely tempted to keep vigil with her, fatigue caught up with me all at once. I climbed the stairs and collapsed in my bunk, falling to sleep almost instantly.

I awoke to rapping on the door to my quarters. It took several repetitions before I had any idea of where I was or how I'd gotten there. Everything after I'd left the wedding seemed like a dream. Down the rabbit hole after a cat with my ring…

Peach-colored light filtered in through the curtains over my window, and I had the strangest impression that I saw a medieval stone tower slide by outside.

Tap-tap-tap!

"Coming," I said, running fingers through my hair, hoping that bedhead looked cute on me. I stood and opened the door and found Dribbler grinning at me.

"Dribbler! You're awake?"

He nodded. "And I'm just fine, thanks to you, sweetie!"

I hugged him. My face smooshed up against his chest; his arms engulfed me. "You'd do the same for me," I murmured, not knowing what else to say.

He let me go and nodded with enthusiasm. "You bet I would! I owe ya. Anyway, we'll be in St. Louis in a few minutes, thought you might want to look around before we get too busy."

"Wait, wait," I protested, "it was night, how is it morning? St. Louis isn't that far away."

Dribbler shrugged. "I guess Zamboni took the long way 'round, to confuse any goons that might have followed us? And I think we stopped for a while somewhere, too? Not sure. I've been out too."

"Did…" I began uncertainly. "Did Hope *make* us go to sleep?"

Dribbler shrugged. "Hope's singing voice can be pretty persuasive. I think it was more a suggestion than anything. Anyway, I trust her not to abuse that power. She cares about everyone."

"Yeah, she does seem to be good to you all," I said.

Dribbler shook his head. "No, dude, not just the crew. Everyone. Hope cares about *everyone*."

I followed him downstairs, and we found the others eating biscuits off of a tray. I picked one up and took a bite, discovering it to have cheese and bacon baked into it. Marcy handed me a lidded cup of coffee, which I sipped with great enthusiasm. I put aside worries about any blisters it might incur on the way down.

I noticed that Hope had not yet joined the rest of the crew.

Marcy held a clipboard and pen, her hair tied up in a bun. Today, she dressed like a disco librarian, wearing a lime green jumpsuit with blue and yellow diagonal stripes, with cat-eye glasses perched up on top of her head. "Okay, we're playing the old New Louie Coliseum. They supply the power, but we have to supply the amps and speakers."

"A whole coliseum? Where do you keep speakers like that on *La Esperanza*?" I asked.

Dribbler touched my shoulder and said, "Remember, my world got knocked back pretty far in the Sixties. Any buildings here older than about 40 years were put together out of the rubble. This isn't like the Fieldhouse or the Stadium in your Indy. It'll hold a couple thousand, tops. Acoustics are fantastic, though."

Marcy went on, "I'd rather not leave the bus unattended, so someone's going to have to work lights and sound, and someone's going to have to work security. Which do you want, Jules?"

I frowned. "A couple thousand people, and there's no security?"

She waved her pen in dismissal. "Oh, they have their own security for the premises, along with box office and all that. I mean, someone's got to have the band's back, especially after that bombing attempt."

I nodded. "I can do either, but I have more experience working boards than cracking skulls."

Miz Davenport smiled as she wrote something on the clipboard. "You're turning out to be a good investment, Jules my dear. That works for me. I have more than tasers up my sleeve, anyway. Jasmine, are you willing to help me out?"

The cat yawned and stretched, then trotted over to Marcy and rubbed up against her ankle, and nodded with a "mrrt!

"Thanks, buddy."

"She saved us all last night," I said. "We might not have found the bomb in time if not for Jasmine's nose."

The cat preened, giving herself an impromptu tongue bath.

Babs scritched behind Jasmine's ears with a fond smile. "Oh, we know we can count on our Jazzy, she's very clever."

After a few more minutes of coffee, biscuits, and conversation, the bus pulled to a halt.

Marcy touched a panel, and the windows became somewhat less opaque. Outside, there appeared to be a row of rough stone buildings set along a smooth concrete street. People meandered up and down sidewalks in their suits, hats, and face masks. Hands on the clock tower across the way from us showed the time to be about a quarter past nine.

Wow, I slept in later than I thought!

Miz Davenport handed out plain white filter masks to each of us. The ramp and stairs whined and descended to the street below. I strapped my mask on and found the material allowed me to breathe much more freely than I expected.

She said, "The masks are more for social interactions than actual danger, but the air is worse here nearer to old St. Louis."

Dribbler added, for my benefit, "Old St. Louis is a crater, a lake in the Mississippi now. The worst washed downstream decades ago, but better safe than sorry, y'know?"

We filed down the stairs and around to the back, which Harlan had opened and rolled out the rear ramp. We stood at a loading dock, where we were met by a stocky woman in a yellow floral business dress with a matching mask. Her ash-blonde hair fell in a thick French braid down her back.

"Miz Fox, I can assure you," said Harlan, "We have no curse words in any of our music. Nothing sexually suggestive for this show. Hope don't like that none, anyhow. Hope's Tour is about uplifting music, an' music that'll make you cry, but in a good way."

"Hmm. That's *Mrs.* Fox if you please! We don't get outlandish folk playing here much, so I will have you know it is only by that reputation you describe that we've allowed this off-world rock and roll show. See that your talent sticks to that reputation, Mister Harper!"

Harlan's brows formed thunderheads, and his face reddened a bit. "Now, see here ma'am—"

Marcy interposed herself. "That will be fine, Mrs. Fox. We're looking forward to playing the Coliseum. Its *reputation* is what drew us here. Very historic, very full of civic pride." With a warning glance to Harlan, she added, "It will be an *honor* to play here."

Mrs. Fox regarded Miz Davenport for a long, tense moment. Then, she extended a gloved hand to Marcy. Marcy accepted. "Very well. Rebecca Fox, Director of the Coliseum."

"Marcy Davenport. Hope's Tour band manager."

Just then, Jasmine skittered into our midst and yowled.

Babs tensed and studied the cat.

I turned around to see what had Jasmine so spooked.

Protesters marched towards us, men and women carrying signs that said, "Fishie Go Home!" and "No Aliens in New Louie!" and "Float Off, Deviants!"

Chapter 6 – 32-20 Blues

"Arch off! Arch off! No aliens! No aliens! Float off! Float off!"

The protesters' chants drew passers-by to join the growing crowd.

Babs hissed in my ear, "Jules, take cover!" and shoved me towards the cargo ramp.

I stumbled but caught myself. Jasmine passed me to zip up in the cargo bay. Babs walked right up to the lead protesters, her arms wide, shouting at them. "Back off!"

Dribbler joined her, waving his hands. "Cool it, dudes! It's okay, I promise. I'm from here, these are good people, they're with me!"

Contrary to Babs' instructions, I took a few paces forward, behind the other two.

Behind me, Miz Davenport raised her voice to be heard over the crowd. "Mrs. Fox! Can you please do something?"

I heard the crackle of a radio; Rebecca Fox shouted, "Security! We've got problems at the loading dock!"

A large man in a brick red suit threw his sign to the pavement and puffed himself up so big, I fully expected buttons to fly off his shirt. "You back off, aliens! You don't belong here!"

Dribbler got up in his face so close, I thought he might bump chests with the guy. "We're just here to put on a show! We're here by request!"

A little elderly woman with a "Devils Go Home!" sign slipped around Dribbler, and I held up my hands, palms towards her, and shook my head. She took a swing at me with the poster board sign, forcing me to jump back a step.

Mrs. Fox appeared at my side, shouting at the crowd in general, asking them to disperse.

The crowd paused, then resumed chanting.

The large man in a brick red suit shoved Dribbler backward into the elderly woman. The woman fell in a heap at my feet, her sign spinning off to hit Mrs. Fox.

Enraged shouts erupted from the crowd, and I heard someone yell, "Aliens knocked that old lady over!"

I leaned down to offer a hand to help the lady up, but she smacked my hand away. Blood trickled down from her nose, staining her polka-dotted mask. She shouted, "Get your floaty paws off of me, you pervert!"

This did not go over at all well with the crowd, who began to advance on us in a line.

Babs became a blur; she kicked a man in the shins and folded a woman in half by punching her in the gut.

Behind me, Marcy shouted at Babs to stop fighting back.

The weight of Marcy's taser in my sweater pocket gave me ideas, but at that moment, all I could do was hold animal terror in check to keep from fleeing in terror. I backed up towards the cargo ramp as Dribbler and Babs were forced to retreat.

Something flew past my head. Another something, too.

Then, stars appeared in the daytime, and my head rang as I sat down hard on the ground without meaning to. Dazed, I scrambled on all fours to get away, and I happened upon a rock half the size of a baseball. A reddish rock. A wet, reddish rock. Half of everything went red, as something hot and wet trickled into my left eye.

Someone stepped on my leg, and I let out a yelp. Someone else screamed at me and brandished a stick with tatters of a sign attached. I cringed and held up my hands to ward off the attack.

Just then, there came a voice of such clarity and intensity that it cut through the terrible din of the rioting mob.

A wonderful, heart-rending voice, weaving a song of such sadness, my heart broke even as the world swam around me.

Darkness crowded in from the edges of my vision, like dark static. As the lights went out, my last sight was of the crowd turning as one to look as Hope stood atop *La Esperanza*, her arms wide, a sun-lit silvery gown blowing back behind her in the wind, like wings.

I awoke to the soft orange glow of a flying saucer hovering over my face. The light bathed my face in warmth and covered my skin with a somewhat pleasant electric tingle. My head throbbed, but my vision focused; the glowing disk couldn't be a flying saucer, because behind it was someone I knew, so it had to be a *tiny* flying saucer or something else entirely.

A gentle song in an alien language accompanied the soft warbling of the healing device. The song rose like a summer breeze; it called out in long notes punctuated by rapid-fire clicking and woodwind-like susurrations. A pair of dark, wide-set, kindly eyes peered at me over a muzzle full of tiny sharp teeth, curved in a merry smile.

Hope's hand caressed my cheek as she sang to me. "Oh Jules, no more catching rocks with your head! You are quite brave, but you aren't invulnerable! You will be fine, but don't scare us like that!"

I couldn't help myself, I giggled. "Mmmph. I'll try not to. Just thought it might make Dribbler feel better if someone else got knocked upside the head."

Hope switched off the device, and cool air washed over my face. I sat up, though this earned me a critical look from Hope.

I found myself alone with Hope in the main cabin of the bus. Well, not completely alone; Zamboni stood nearby, holding a medical bag so Hope could stow the healing disk.

Maybe she read my thoughts. "The rest of the crew are surveying the Coliseum. The protesters left, and Rebecca Fox has promised us her security will keep them at a distance if they should return. You should rest another hour or so before joining them."

"How long have I been out?"

"Oh, not too long, maybe twenty minutes? Part of that was my doing, I didn't want you moving around before I had you checked for a concussion."

I started to climb to my feet. "But the lights and sound—"

Hope placed a gentle hand on my shoulder and guided me to sit back down. She finished my sentence for me. "—are in the capable hands of Harlan and Dribbler. You can join them soon enough. Now, my friend, you should rest, or perhaps sleep."

No compulsion accompanied her singing voice this time, as far as I could tell, but remembering the size of the rock that hit me, I decided to take her advice.

Hope stood and told me she needed to warm up for the show. She gave some instructions to Zamboni, then slipped out the door.

Zamboni stepped towards me with that funny three-footed gait. He handed me a bottle of water. I thanked him and sipped from it. At that moment, the icy cold water seemed like the best thing I'd ever tasted.

The robot stood nearby, as enigmatic as ever. I decided to attempt a conversation with him again. "Hey, Zamboni."

The robot replied, "Greetings, Jules."

"Where do you come from?"

Zamboni paused a moment before answering, "I am from a world designated by the Arch authority as 'Zetta Prime'."

"What's Zetta Prime like?"

Zamboni said, "It is like your Beta Earth, but with most technologies far in advance, and far fewer humans."

Intrigued, I asked, "Are there many other robots there like yourself?"

The robot paused long enough for me to consider repeating my question, but answered, "There are more artificial life forms such as myself in Zetta Prime than there are humans. No two Zetta Prime artificial life forms are alike, in the way that no two humans are alike. Each has his own form and consciousness."

I'll admit, I'm sensitive where gender and pronouns are concerned, so I had to ask. "You say 'Each has *his* own form'. Do you mean to say all artificial life forms are referred to with male pronouns?"

"No. In that case, 'his' was used as a generic pronoun. Many so-called robots are designated with feminine or neutral pronouns. Lesser intelligences are often referred to as 'it'. I chose masculine pronouns for myself in my first year of activation."

Impressed, I said, "That's fantastic! I have chosen they/them pronouns for myself. Do you understand that designation?"

"Yes. I will use that designation for you in the future, Jules Martin."

"Thank you, Zamboni."

Our warm moment over, the robot had no reply, so he returned to guarding the door to the bus.

I drowsed for an hour but became fidgety and tried standing up and pacing around the cabin. Nothing wibbled or wobbled in a way that it shouldn't, so I ventured outside. When I caught sight of people walking around, I remembered to don my mask.

At the rear of *La Esperanza*, I encountered Dribbler rolling his drum kit down the ramp on a dolly. Once his burden sat on level ground, he fussed over me, examining the side of my head with concern.

I blushed at the close attention but waved him off. "I'm fine, I'm fine! Thanks to Hope and her healing gadget."

We worked together to unload more gear to transport into the Coliseum. I don't know about Dribbler, but despite the presence of Coliseum security, it made me feel safer than working alone. Once I had the sound cables unloaded, I even asked Babs to help me unreel them, though I could have done it by myself nearly as fast.

The Coliseum did not try to hide its origins; its walls and tiered levels had been fashioned of cemented-together concrete chunks and other rubble. Despite this patchwork look, it had been in use for decades, and walkways had worn smooth with decades of enthusiastic use. Wooden benches, as well as a few fancier box seats, lined these tiers around most of the structure. The ground level had still more wooden benches and a few concession stands, reminding me a bit of a renaissance faire.

The stage at the New Louie Coliseum stood at one end of the inner oval on ground level. A curved metal scaffolding arched over the stage; a rectangular metal grid hung suspended by the arch by an array of many steel cables. Can lights, a couple of spotlights, and a boom mic hung from the grid, as well as Harlan. The stage manager crawled around on top of the grid, adjusting light angles and inserting gels.

The crew knew their routine well. Setup went so smoothly that anything I thought to do to help put me in the way of someone else. So, once the sound/light boards had been placed off in a corner of the stage, I worked on sound checks and familiarized myself with all the sliders and switches on the boards.

Miz Davenport equipped me with a headset and a two-foot-long flashlight. She and I did coms checks and went over the various signals for stage directions I might get from Harlan and Babs. Then she told me about the flashlight's special features.

"This has settings. Setting One is a red light, so you can see the boards without messing up any dark vision you might have, and without drawing much attention to yourself. Setting Two is a high beam flood that you can use if we lose power. Setting Three is a powerful laser pointer, in case you need to direct my attention somewhere. And don't use Setting Four."

"What's Setting Four do?"

"It's a flash burst, a directed beam of a few million candlepower. A few pulses of that will drain the battery quickly. It's meant for self-defense, to blind an attacker. Honestly, if anyone gets close enough for that to matter, you'll want to use Setting Zero."

I turned the flashlight over in my hands, looking for Setting Zero. "I don't see any—"

Marcy took the flashlight from me and smacked it into her opposite palm with a grin. "Setting Zero is using this bad boy like a nightstick. But please, don't cave anyone's head in, no matter how aggressive they may be. We don't need a PR nightmare like that, okay?"

I took the flashlight as she handed it back to me. "Got it. Flash 'em, bash 'em, but don't trash 'em."

Marcy smiled and ruffled my hair. "You got it, kiddo. Oh, also, keep chatter on the com to a minimum, and if you can help it, keep your voice down, Jasmine's ears are super sensitive."

"You mean, Jazzy's got a—"

On cue, the cat hopped up on the chair next to me, wearing a cat-sized headset. She stood tall and prim, chin up, with what looked to me like a smug expression.

We went through more checks, including a dress rehearsal. Babs laid down a throaty bassline, accompanying Dribbler's driving beat. Hope appeared, escorted by Jasmine, and she picked up the mic and sang Eric Clapton's "Layla".

The chill air of Gamma Earth rose several degrees as Hope belted out the song; she nearly had me on my knees by the end, my insides melting like butter on her tongue. I wondered if the others ever got used to the power of Hope's singing.

I hoped I never would.

After that one song, Hope left the stage to pick her wardrobe for the performance. Babs and Dribbler noodled around with their instruments. Dribbler surprised me by jamming on an electric guitar while Babs switched to harmonica and then keyboards during their practice sets. Marcy even stood in for Hope on a couple of songs, and while she couldn't match the magnitude of Hope's voice, I felt certain she could front a band on her own merit.

Babs rolled her synth keyboard over to my sound/light booth and pointed out some programmed effects and backing rhythms I could add if I felt comfortable. After we went over the effects, I surprised *them* by playing a little Professor Longhair that I'd picked up at one time. Terribly out of practice, I flushed with embarrassment compared to the professionals' performance, but I got a round of applause from the crew and a few Coliseum security people nearby.

Hours passed that way. Then, all at once, people filed into the Coliseum. An electric tension built as the seats filled with people in suits, dresses, hats, and masks. The murmur of their conversations built an almost tangible wall around us. As we called out last-minute directions to each other over the coms, I smiled with the thrill of being a part of something much bigger than myself.

The tension built to a crescendo, and then at Babs' signal, I lowered the house lights all around the Coliseum, leaving us all in the reddish twilight of the setting sun. After a dramatic pause, I raised the slider for the spotlight centered on the lonely mic in the center of the stage.

That was Hope's cue to appear.

She didn't.

Babs and Dribbler stalled on bass and drums.

Jasmine yowled over the coms. Harlan cursed, backstage somewhere out of sight. Marcy called out something unintelligible, and I knew something had gone wrong.

Chapter 7 – Phonograph Blues

My spotlight blazed a circle in the middle of the stage that should have been full of Hope. The coms fell silent.

But other sounds rose around me.

First of all, the crowd murmur sharpened, and individual shouts reached my ears, full of irritation, even anger. These people wanted a show, and they wanted it *now*.

I glared out into the dark at the attendees. I wondered how many of them would have sided with the protesters this morning. I wondered how many of those were among the loudmouths calling for Hope to perform for them at their whim.

Jasmine the cat leaped up onto my console. She yowled at my face, the mournful sound echoing in my ear on the com channel.

"What is it, Jazzy?"

Her eyes looked at me, wide and wild; her tail stood up and trembled. She jerked her chin back toward the loading dock and our tour bus. Then, she jumped down and dashed off in that direction.

I stood up, frozen in indecision for a long moment.

Dribbler toed his bass drum, starting a low, slow beat that gained momentum; the beats came faster and louder, building. The audience cheered, stoked by this sign of the show starting, and began to clap and stomp along.

My gaze shifted from Dribbler to Babs, who stepped into the spotlight and shouted, "Good evening, New Louie! How ya doin'?"

They were stalling. I had to take this opportunity to go figure out what had gone wrong. I stuck the big flashlight in my belt and dashed backstage after Jasmine.

As I ran, I heard Babs' rich, smoky voice fill the Coliseum with a song in Spanish that I didn't recognize. She accompanied herself on guitar with a catchy blues riff. Dribbler provided a bass beat line and teased with brushes on cymbals.

When we emerged onto the loading dock, our bus wasn't there. Our dollies, ropes, tarps, winches, and packing materials lay all around, discarded.

Jasmine howled and hissed. I scanned the parking lot, searching the deepening gloom to see what she wanted me to see.

Once I saw it, I couldn't figure out how I'd missed it. Out beyond the entry arch, *La Esperanza* wove around the gravel lot surrounding the Coliseum, spraying stones and dust in its wake.

An improbable machine pursued the tour bus. To my eyes, it looked like a stagecoach with two tall, jointed mechanical legs. It ran like a giant ostrich. Each of its hopping steps covered the length of a Honda Civic. Smoke or steam belched out from a chimney on top, and someone hung out the window with a bell-muzzled rifle. Was that a musket?

Something like ball lightning arced out from the end of the rifle and sizzled through the air. Electric tendrils exploded across the bus's metal skin. *La Esperanza* shuddered and the engines whined, but it kept rolling.

Boom-boom-boom! came the amplified thunder of Dribbler's bass drum, echoing off the insides of the Coliseum behind me.

Someone popped up out of the hatch on top of the tour bus; the crack of a proper rifle shot fired back at the mechanical monstrosity.

A groan came from below. I tore my eyes from the unfolding drama between *La* Esperanza and the strange assault vehicle. Marcy lay sprawled among the equipment and materials, half-covered by a padded tarp.

I jumped down from the loading dock and called her name. "Miz Davenport! Marcy! Are you okay?"

Jasmine bounded over to Marcy and licked her face a few times.

Marcy moaned and rolled her head to gaze at me, eyes unfocused. "Jules? Why… why did you do it?"

Relieved, but confused, I shook my head. "I had to come see what happened after the shouting on the coms. Babs is stalling on stage."

She closed her eyes and opened them and focused on me this time. "Not that. I mean, *this*. You know," she made a vague hammering motion with one hand. Then she frowned. "But you're not a girl, are you, Jules?"

"What? No, not a girl. I'm just me. What are you talking about? What's with the giant steampunk robot thing out there? What happened to Coliseum security?"

She tried to rotate her head around to watch the chase going on out in the lot. More gunshots rang out. She looked back at me and said, "Thought you'd know. Guess I'm seeing things. Those guys ran when the portal opened. Almost don't blame 'em."

Jasmine yowled again, and I looked at her. "Right. First things first. Let's see what we can do to help. Hold tight, Miz Davenport!"

Marcy pulled the tarp over her like a drunk nursing a hangover.

I scooped up some tie-down straps and ratchets and began work on the archway.

The bus and the ostrich-coach disappeared from view. I called out on the coms, "Harlan! You there?"

The crack of a rifle reported over the com before I heard it echo from somewhere out around the bend of the Coliseum. Harlan shouted, "Kinda busy here, y'all!"

I kept my voice calm and even. "Can you come on back to the loading dock?"

Harlan growled, "Could do, but ah don't think I feel like gettin' trapped just now!"

"I've got an idea."

"Best be a damn good idea!"

"Trust me?"

"Fine. See you soon. Best be ready."

One end securely tied, I played the straps across the width of the arch, daisy-chained together with ratchets. I looped this end around the other side of the big steel-and-concrete archway. I stopped short of pulling it tight, letting the straps lay slack in the dust.

Harlan called out over the coms to let me know they were coming around. I pulled out my flashlight and stood in the middle of the archway. I switched it to setting two, the high-beam, and swung it back and forth in the dusty air like a small searchlight.

The bus barreled into view and turned so hard towards me, I thought it might tip over. Instead, the backend fishtailed around and I found myself in the way of the rather large bus. It grew closer every second; its engines thrummed in time with my pounding heartbeat.

I held the flashlight straight up, illuminating my face from below as I timed my next move. The bus loomed larger and louder, and I took a gasping breath and leaped to one side, rolling on my shoulders to spring up in a crouch just to one side as it roared past me. The bus's brakes screamed as gravel churned beneath its tires as it approached the loading dock much too fast.

I left that for Harlan and Hope to figure out.

As the back end of the bus revealed the ostrich-coach, I used the setting three laser to sight on the front windows of the coach. A woman in a dusty leather coat and hat hung out the side and aimed at me with a bell-muzzled rifle.

Then I switched the big flashlight to setting four.

The light of the sun at noon blasted out of the hefty flashlight in my hands. I gripped the handle tighter, as though the power of the beam could wrest the handle from my grasp. The light splashed off the front of the assault vehicle, and it wobbled.

The whole scene plunged into eye-dazzled darkness as time ran out on setting four.

The thing creaked, groaned, and swayed in such a way that made me fear for my life, and I had to dodge out of the way of the giant metal feet as they slammed down where I'd stood only a moment before. For another terrible moment, I feared the blinded driver might somehow slam on the brakes, bringing the thing to a halt, and ruining my plan.

But Newton was on my side, and the thing's momentum kept it careening forward, clawed feet thudding and scrabbled in the gravel. But it was too late.

I shuffled sideways out of its way and backed up. I kicked my toe under the strap, lifted it to my chest, and hauled its length aloft, the other end held fast by the archway.

One terrifying foot lifted and the straps caught it in mid-stride.

The walking machine swayed and lurched forward. With a terrible metal groan, it lost its footing and came crashing down, face-planted into the gravel below. My ears ached from the tremendous cacophony.

A fire broke out in an instant. The scents of kerosene and campfire accompanied a wave of heat that washed over me.

On the other side of the growing inferno, Harlan dashed from the open backside of the tour bus, right into the disaster. He still carried his rifle, and also dragged a tarp behind him as he ran.

Despite my fear of flames and potential explosion, I ran towards him, and as we converged, a figure crawled from the wreckage. The woman who'd been firing the strange weapon hunched under her thick coat as she crawled away. One leg dragged behind her at a disturbing angle, and I decided it must be broken.

Harlan grabbed one of her arms and yelled at me over the roar of the fire, "Help me!"

I took her other arm and we dragged her away from the wreckage as fast as we could. The cool night air of Gamma Earth caressed my face and filled my lungs.

WHOOMPH!

The rest of the ruined vehicle's fuel went up in a massive yellow-green plume of flame; the concussion knocked us all to the ground. My head swam as if in a dream, and I lost track of my bearings and time for more than a few seconds.

When I came to myself again, the woman stood on one foot above me, and with a shock, I knew her face.

In my confusion, all I could stutter out was, "It's... it's you! What are you doing?"

Then I saw that she held an odd sort of pistol in her hand. It ended in a wide bell, just like her sci-fi musket had. I thought sure she'd do me in right then, but instead, she turned away from the fire and pointed the gun outward and an intensely bright blue fireball spun out to hover a few feet away. The ball widened and expanded into an electric blue oval, like a standing mirror. In the middle of the oval was another world. Sunlight shone through the hole in space, and the woman stumbled towards it.

"Stop! Wait!" called Harlan, struggling to get up on all fours.

She hopped through the portal and turned to give me a weak smile. "We'll meet again, I promise you."

Before either Harlan or I could get to our feet, the portal irised down to a painful point of light, which winked out.

Harlan and I stared at each other, catching our breath.

I stammered, "Harlan! That was... I mean, it wasn't, but it *was—*"

Harlan's eyes were grim as he nodded. "Yep. I reckon that was you, Jules. And I know where she's from, too."

"Harlan, what do you mean?" I said, breathless. "Where is she from? That version of me, I mean. How do you know?"

Harlan stood silhouetted by the backdrop of the fiery wreckage. "Well, I reckon she's from my home 'verse, or thereabouts. I know 'cause that there," he said, jerking a thumb back at the ruined walking coach, "is a 'babayaga'. A war machine the Kansan Empire uses to get soldiers and important folk through the hills and badlands. Ain't never seen 'em anywhere but back home on Erde."

I blinked. "Erde?"

"My 'verse. It's not like yours, or even this place. There never was a 'United States' of anything. Just a bunch of smaller countries squabblin' and warrin' over North America. But we can't stand here yappin' about that right now. We gotta check in on Hope, and the show."

Even as he said her name, Hope appeared on the ramp of the bus, wearing a shimmering metallic green gown draped with a shawl made of netting and rhinestones. Her face was hidden behind a blue-green veil. She beckoned to us, and Harlan and I made our careful way over to her. Sirens blared in the distance.

Hope offered a mitten-hand to Harlan, and the two shook and held each other's gaze a long moment. She said, "I don't pay you enough, do I, Harlan?"

He chuckled and replied, "No' ma'am. But I'd do it all for free if I didn't have so many damn debts to pay."

Hope's laughter came out full of squeaks and clicks. "Well, add this debt to *my* tab then, Mister Harper! Well done."

She let go of his hand and turned her attention to me. She took two steps, closing the distance to mere inches between us. She raised her arms to embrace me, then stopped. "May I?"

Her sudden close presence overwhelmed me such that all I could do was nod my consent.

The netting and gauzy material of her gown enveloped me, and I found myself wrapped up in Hope. I put my arms around her body and held her at first as though she might break. She squeezed me tight, and I realized that I was the more fragile of the two of us.

She half-whispered, half sang into my ear. "Thank you, Jules. Your quick thinking saved Harlan, Zamboni, and me. I won't forget this." My skin tingled everywhere she touched me, while my heart pounded a beat better than Dribbler's bass drum.

Not good with this kind of attention, I changed the subject. "Miz Davenport, she's hurt. Can you see to her?"

Before she let me go, Hope brushed her veiled muzzle across my cheek. "Of course."

My face burned with some strong emotion I couldn't identify as the three of us made our way to where Marcy lay cocooned in tarps. Jasmine sat atop her, standing guard.

Hope touched Marcy's face as she passed the high-tech healing frisbee over her body. The tension left Marcy's body, and she peered past Hope to look at me. "That' wasn't you, was it, Jules?"

I shook my head. "I saw her too. I guess she's the Jules from Harlan's world."

Marcy's mouth formed an "O" of surprise. She peered up at Harlan. "Erde? Really?"

Harlan shrugged. "Most likely. Don't know how, but someone there can make a portal open over here in Gamma. Shortest route I know, we'd have to go through five arches to get there."

Hope murmured, "Those are just the established routes. My people can skip from world to world with our verseships. It's how I ended up Delta, far, far from my home on poor lost Tristel."

"Y'all crashed there, I heard you say once," said Harlan.

Hope didn't answer that, but said, "Certainly the Arches follow the most stable paths, and carry the least risk. But there are other ways."

Something in the tone of her voice kept me from asking any questions about her home, or the crash. Harlan fell silent, and Marcy closed her eyes and rested.

Fire engines arrived and began putting out the flaming wreckage behind us. Steam wreathed us as Hope sang a soothing song while she tended to Marcy.

Dribbler's voice burst from the com in my ear, startling me. "Hey, are you all alive out there? Babs is doin' great, but the Gammans are getting' restless. They want Hope, and we can't stall much longer."

"There was an attack, Dribs," I replied over the air. "Marcy's hurt and all of us are shaken up pretty bad. Maybe we should—"

Hope interrupted me with an uncharacteristic snap. "No. I'll go onstage. Harlan, you know enough to take it from here," she said, handing the healing saucer to our stage manager.

He nodded, and said, "Show must go on. I gotcha."

Before I could object further, Hope took my hand and we trotted back into the Coliseum, toward the backstage.

Dribbler called out over the coms, fear tinging his voice. "Jules? Marcy's hurt? What's going on?"

Struggling to keep up with Hope, I said, "Stand by. Hope and I are on our way. Marcy will be okay."

I swear I heard Dribbler groan. "The show must go on, huh?"

"That's what Harlan said, too."

"That's Hope for you, dude."

As we approached the curtains, Hope gave my hand a final squeeze and we parted ways. I took up my post at the control boards as Babs gave way to Hope, introducing her with a flourish.

She cried out, "Gentlefolk of the New Louie Coliseum, it is my great pleasure to give you our interdimensional diva, Hope the Tristellian!"

I widened the spotlight to take in both women and then narrowed it in to focus tight and bright on Hope. The shimmers of her dress covered the crowd in waves of green, as though they watched from beneath the ocean. The sparkles of her rhinestone-covered netting played bright points of light all around the Coliseum, as though the stars had come down to rest among them.

The applause was underwhelming; this crowd had to be won over. I figured they'd been kept waiting too long, and more than that, they didn't like off-worlders. And Hope was likely the most off-world person they'd ever encountered.

Hope opened up with a blues-rock version of Abba's "Take a Chance on Me". Not a combination I would have thought of, but with her sweet alien voice and Bab's masterful guitar and Dribbler's irresistible beat, the song had me wanting to sing along. I played colorful lights across the stage, hoping to evoke a muted disco vibe to go with the genre-mashup song.

Somewhat more enthusiastic applause broke out at the end, but Hope gave them no time to breathe as she launched into "Black Friday Rule", one of my personal favorites by Flogging Molly. Babs and Dribbler drove home the rhythm while Hope spun the song's story. Her voice soared and nearly broke my heart as it spoke of missing a home far away and out of reach.

During that song, Marcy appeared in the corner of my view, hovering in the wings of the stage. She held a shotgun across her body, eyes narrow and burning as she peered out over the crowd. I'd been so lost in the music that I hadn't been keeping a lookout as well as I should have. I thanked what luck I had left for my lapse not costing us anything. This time.

"All clear," called out Harlan over the coms. "Fire's out. Marcy's on her feet, and I'm havin' a word with Mrs. Fox about her so-called security team."

"Copy that," I replied. "Show's underway, no technical difficulties. Tough crowd, though."

I almost laughed as Hope segued into the next song, the Talking Heads classic "Burning Down the House". Only Hope could sing that song with a slow, bluesy, even sultry delivery. She cast her musical spell like a seductive net across the whole of the Coliseum; if these Gammans could resist her, I didn't want to know them. As for me, I was caught up and bewitched.

Hope, Babs, and Dribbler let the music trail off and die so that the only sound in the whole Coliseum was that of the crowd. To my astonishment, their applause *still* felt stiff and forced. Why had they even come to see Hope's Tour?

"I can see we need to bring it up a notch," said Hope, breathing hard as she paused. "Maybe it's time I introduced us."

Hope swept an arm to take in Dribbler and his drum set. "On drums, the incomparable master of rhythm, Gamma Earth's own James 'Dribbler' Macgowan!"

A smattering of applause rippled through the stands, along with a few irreverent catcalls. Dribbler mugged for the crowd and filled the air with his percussive wizardry.

"On bass and electric guitar, your hostess for the evening is the amazing Babs Delgado!" Hope swept her other arm to take in the guitarist, who played a complicated riff to show off her chops.

The crowd clapped dutifully and gave Babs a few cheers and whistles.

"Let's have a hand for our stage crew, Harlan Harper the Third, Marcy Davenport, and introducing Jules Martin!

While I appreciated the gesture, having my name spoken by an alien musical goddess to this crowd made me want to crawl under the boards and hide. My face burned as hot as the babayaga had out front, and as I searched for a place to hide, Jasmine peered back up at me as if to tell me that she wouldn't let me get away with it.

Hope continued. "People of Gamma Earth, I'm Hope, and this is my Tour! We're glad to be here, and we hope you're having a great time! Now, if you will indulge me for a while, please let me sing you a song of my people. Mister Macgowan, won't you start our special song?"

Dribbler saluted her with his sticks and dragged a wire brush across the edge of his cymbals in a dirge-like rhythm, the effect sounding to my ears like heavy chains clattering. To this, he added a rat-tata-rat-tata-rat-tata beat on the snare.

Babs joined in with a twangy guitar that belonged in rock and roll from the fifties.

Hope sang into the mic, and I couldn't believe I heard her sing those words.

No. She couldn't be doing *that* song. How could she even *know* that song? A song only played around Halloween, at least in my world.

As she went on, it couldn't be any other song. The crowd rippled with applause and delight, and as she launched into the first chorus, Hope ripped off her veil and screamed!

I leaned into a mic and joined Babs and Dribbler in singing backup. "She did the mash!"

"I did the monster mash!" cried Hope.

I laughed and played some muted sound effects of bubbling cauldrons and ghostly moans as the song went on. The crowd ate it up, and I guessed Bobby "Boris" Pickett's perennial novelty song must have come out just before The Big One blew everything up on Gamma Earth. Maybe this made the silly song even more memorable to the people here, having waded through war, famine, and pestilence to crawl back to where they'd been beforehand?

She'd taken a big risk, but Hope managed to win the crowd over with that one. She went on to rock the house with covers of George Thorogood, Bessie Smith, and even The Mamas and the Papas. As things wound down, she took another risk and offered them the choice of having her sing a song from her home 'verse.

The crowd went wild, cheering and clapping for more.

Hope sat down for the first time since she'd taken the stage, and I dimmed the spotlight just a bit and brought up deep blue background lights to accentuate the green of her dress.

Dribbler put down his sticks, and Babs bowed her head, letting Hope sing her final song *a capella*.

She began with a long, mournful whistling, rising like steam in a teakettle. She accompanied that warbling tone with clicks and a keening that rose from deep within her. Hope unleashed the raw emotion in a musical howl that shook the Coliseum to its foundation. She paused for breath, and I held my own breath, along with the entire crowd.

The trilling language from her homeworld tumbled out of Hope. I had no frame of reference; nothing resembling individual words came from her mouth, but the emotion behind the sounds rang true and clear.

I had never heard a sound so lonely or lost as the song that Hope gave us all that night. I wept, there behind the electronic boards, for everyone to see. In other circumstances, I'd be too afraid to cry in public. But Hope had everyone here, several thousand of us, caught up in her spell; as deep as that lonely feeling reached inside me, I knew I wasn't alone in my tears.

And then, at the very end of her song, Hope let her voice rise, just a little. Just enough to let a ray of sunshine reach the bottom of the ocean of her sadness. I turned up the warmth on the spotlight, adding golden light to the pool surrounding her. Her voice rose in strength and pitch, and she gave us all a bit of her namesake; she ended her song by giving us hope.

"Okay, that's the show," came Harlan's voice over the com. "Cut the spot, bring up the house lights."

I worked the light board as he directed but couldn't help myself. I said, "That's it? She's all done?"

"Remember," he said, "she doesn't do encores. Always leave 'em wanting more, she says. Now, let's get packed up, we've got to hit the road for Delta Earth."

"We're not even staying the night here?"

Harlan growled. "Well, that was the plan, but since that attack by your double from my 'verse, we gotta move on. Might not be up to me, but I figure it might be time to go pay a visit back home to see what's what."

Chapter 9 – Hellhound on My Trail

"So, what's the plan?" I asked after we'd packed up and made a hasty exit from the New Louie Coliseum. Sitting in the common area on the tour bus, I rather enjoyed being sandwiched between Hope and Dribbler. Jasmine the cat paced the back of the seat behind me, then leaped several feet to the other couch.

Harlan sat across from us with Marcy and Babs, seeming older than I remembered. "That's up to the boss, but if it were up to me, we'd skitter across Delta and on into Achse before sunrise."

Hope sighed. "Are we in such a rush?"

"Aren't we, ma'am?" Harlan sat up straighter and knit his fingers together in his lap. "I reckon two attempts to kill you in Gamma is plenty of reason to hurry. And Jules' pretty twin from my home 'verse brought out the big guns opening a portal to get at us like that. We can't sit still and wait for the next attack."

"Sure," said Babs, throwing her hands in the air. "Why wait for the next one, when we can run right to where the assassin came from! May as well make it easy on them, hmmm?"

Marcy shook her head with enough violence that her dangling earrings flew out to the sides. "No, you don't get it, Babs. We go there. We find out who's behind this. And then, we stop them. Harlan's right, we have to move quickly. Be unpredictable."

"But then we can't go to Erde," said Dribbler, leaning forward to hold out his right-hand palm upwards. "If you were them, where would you guess we'd go? I mean, where else? Then all they gotta do is lay traps for us the whole way there." He ticked off his fingers one at a time. Achse, League, Arne, then Erde. Boom, boom, boom!"

Hope nodded and sang, "We shall have to do what we can to be unpredictable, my friends. But I fear we must do as Harlan says, and go to his homeworld to find out the truth behind these attacks."

I spoke up. "But why would anyone want to attack Hope? Just because she's—"

I paused, uncertain of a good way to finish that sentence. Hope turned towards me, and as her eyes met mine, I felt my face grow hot. I had a sudden wish for the ability to open portals as my doppelganger had; I wanted very much to disappear right that moment.

Hope smiled and touched my face with her soft, smooth hand. Her dark eyes twinkled with amusement. "Jules, you speak out of kindness," she sang. "You have a beautiful soul. Not all would know you by that soul but would see your electric blue hair first. Some would judge you by that because it makes you stand out as different. Many see me as a monster for being more closely related to your dolphins than to humans."

"But you're so beautiful!" I blurted out. "And kind, and you sing like an angel! What threat are you to anyone?"

Harlan grumbled. "Folks'll do stupid things out of fear. And folks are afraid of anything they don't understand."

"Like the protesters in New Louie," said Babs. "Regular people, ready to sharpen their pitchforks just because foreigners came to town to play a show."

"I think someone put them up to that," said Dribbler. "I mean, we'd only just rolled in."

Zamboni's robot voice buzzed over the intercom. "Warning. We will pass through the Arch momentarily. Traversal will take an apparent thirty-seven minutes."

Hope looked past me to speak to Dribbler. "I agree. Though the spark was there already, perhaps fanned to flames by a more deliberate effort. We must resort to subterfuge."

I sighed. "How do we fool an unknown attacker who can see us coming four or five worlds away?"

Hope smiled. "By doing the last thing our attacker expects," she said, turning her head to look at Marcy.

Marcy's eyes widened and she shook her head. "You don't mean it. We can't—"

Harlan slapped his hands together and guffawed. "Don't that beat all? Ma'am, you're my kind of crazy."

Confused, I asked, "Did I miss something? What are we going to do that they won't expect?"

Babs rubbed her face with both hands, then peered through her fingers at Hope. "Ay yi yi. 'The show must go on'?"

Hope smiled and nodded. Jasmine hopped up into her lap and nuzzled her.

Dribbler laughed out loud.

A shimmering, rippling wall passed through the room; Dribbler's laugh stretched like taffy, becoming a drawn-out cackle that belonged in a horror movie. We'd passed into the space between 'verses.

No one spoke for a minute or two as we unscrambled our thoughts. For myself, I had an instantaneous hallucination of Sam and Patrick yelling at each other at a wedding. My wedding, the one I'd fled. It had to be long over, so the vision had to be my mind playing games with me as we passed through the Arch.

"Marcy, tell me about our next gig," said Hope.

"Weeeell, if we keep to plan, it'd be up in Chicago tomorrow night. But that's published and advertised. If we keep that date, we'll still be super predictable. The Arch there goes to Achse, even."

Babs made a face. "I hate that place. And they hate me there, too, for who I am and the color of my skin. Couldn't we go, I don't know, *anywhere* else?"

"Fucking *fascists*!" Dribbler spat the word out with such disgust that Jasmine leaped from Hope's lap and fled the room.

Harlan cast his eyes to the floor. "Not everyone in any 'verse is the same. There are folk like you and me there, too."

Dribbler rubbed his face with both hands and said, "I know, I know. But it's still a bad place. Probably arrest us if we played a show."

Hope nodded to Babs but addressed Dribbler's outburst. "I know. It isn't on our musical tour, for that reason. I doubt the Axis government would allow most of our setlist, and I refuse to sing their songs honoring their 'glorious leadership'."

I'd heard things about Achse, even though it was a couple of hops away from Beta Earth. "Are we going to the Nazi 'verse? I, uh, I don't think they'd take kindly to someone like me. Not that Gamma's been all that friendly."

Dribbler sighed. "Yeah, sorry about that. That's the reason I left this place originally. You'll like Delta though. It's colorful if you understand me."

Marcy said, "We don't have a tour date in Achse. Or League, or Arne, for that matter. The plan was to go on to Alpha. What are you proposing, Hope?"

Hope looked up at the ceiling and was silent for a long moment. Then, she said, "I'm not sure yet, Marcy. If we can obtain something I left in Delta, we may be able to lose our pursuit after we pass through the gate, but it will be a risk. I doubt we'll make our date in Alpha, though I have a feeling we'll end up there eventually. Can you postpone?"

Marcy pursed her lips, and I could almost hear the gears turning as she worked on the problem. "Yes, but won't that be tipping our hand?"

Hope smiled. "Just send the message right before we exit. If my plan works out, they won't' be able to follow. If not, then they're going to have their own troubles in Achse."

Marcy nodded. "Okay, I'll work with that." Her face remained clouded with emotion.

Babs asked Marcy, "Everything okay, *chica*?"

Marcy stared at her hands. "Well, it's just… I hate to bring up uncomfortable things, but it seems important that we talk about Jules' double. Why would another Jules have it in for Hope?"

My face warmed as I realized all eyes in the room focused on me. Jasmine rubbed up against my legs, and I petted her, grateful for the reassurance. "I assure you; I have no idea. I've never even met another one of myself. I'm pretty surprised that she was a she, to be honest, but I guess there are differences between 'verses, even if she's the same person on some level."

Harlan cleared his throat and said, "Can't say I've met any people like you back home. That is, everyone's just a man, or they're a woman, you know."

I shrugged. "Just because the gender binary is more enforced in your 'verse, doesn't mean there aren't people like me. They're just forced into one role or another. It's shocking that another me got involved like that, I can't think what the connection could be. And it does seem to be too incredible to be a coincidence. But why? And why your 'verse, Harlan?"

Harlan shook his head. "Can't say I know. Erde has some connections to Alpha, I suppose. Both 'verses came up with interdimensional travel independently, it seems."

Marcy spoke up. "I understand that there's been some competition between them for multiverse commerce, and a lot of fighting over rights to the Arch Network. They're linked by several instances of the same person: Dionne Sutton."

I said, "She's pretty famous. I saw a special on 'The Dionnes' a month or so ago, with interviews from each. They're all super-geniuses. The Dionne from Beta isn't into physics or quantum computing, she's an environmental scientist devoted to reversing global warming. Beta's more screwed that way than the other Earths, so I'm glad she's putting her mind to it."

Harlan nodded. "Anyways, Erde's got its wars, and those are escalatin' with technology comin' in from other worlds. My country there, the U.S. of Dixie, launched an invasion of the 'verse next door, called Arne, a few years back. Arch Network cut them off and left their army without supplies, so they surrendered. The Atlanta gate opened up again after some negotiations, but the Dixieans haven't forgotten or forgiven."

Dribbler threw his hands in the air. "So, what are you saying, dude? That hotheads in the U.S. of D. in Erde want Hope dead because of a grudge with the Arch Network? You know she's got nothin' to do with that!"

Harlan held up his hands. "Hold on there, son! I don't claim to know anything. I'm an ex-pat. I bugged out after we surrendered to Arne. Couldn't go back, I was too ashamed. I'm just sayin' that's what people are hot about back home, that's all."

"Boys, boys," said Babs. "Keep your cool. We're all friends here, no?"

Dribbler and Harlan started to retort at the same time but Hope interceded. She sang, "What threat am I? I come from a faraway alien 'verse. My people mastered the Ways without permanent portals. We swam the Ways in our ships the way *La Esperanza* makes her way through city streets and highways. Not only am I an outsider, which is frightening enough, but I remind them that their technology can be surpassed by others."

I snorted. "So, they'd kill you for that? Being a reminder?"

Hope touched her snout with both flipper-hands in what I took to be her version of a shrug. "Perhaps. Powerful people do not like such reminders."

"But the Dionnes all seemed so nice, so altruistic," I said, sadness welling up inside me.

Marcy shook her head. "The Dionnes are scientists, not businesswomen. They made interdimensional travel possible, others co-opted the technology. It's they who may feel threatened. This doesn't explain how your doppelganger got involved. Or the synchronicity of you joining our crew not long before she appeared."

Hope looked from Marcy to me, then sang, "Jules, I want you to know, I don't hold you in any way responsible. But if you should get some special insight into her motives, would please let us all know?"

I nodded. "Believe me, it's going to be hard to think of much else until I can figure it out. Putting myself into her place isn't easy, since

I know nothing about her, and not much about Erde. If she's anything like me, she's drifted from thing to thing, picking up skills here, making contacts there. I've never wanted to enlist in the military or any big cause. I'm not a violent person, so I can't picture wanting to kill anyone like that. Something extreme must have happened to push her to do that. I sure don't have the power to open portals, and I don't have access to war machines like that babayaga!"

"Know who *does* have access to portal technology and machines like that?" said Dribbler. "The Arch Network Authority."

Dribbler and Marcy exchanged a long look, then Marcy said, "I hope you're wrong. I don't know how we fight a corporation like that. And forgive me, Hope, but it's not like we could just go underground. You're already too famous, and there aren't any other Tristellians within the network."

Hope stood up and put her arms out to take us all in with a sweeping gesture. She sang, "That, my crew, is why we shall have to go *outside* the network!"

Chapter 10 – Love in Vain

We passed out of the Arch into Delta Earth sometime after midnight. Zamboni let us know that the drive up to Chicago from St. Louis would be about 5 hours. Marcy recommended that we all get some sleep and that we'd be staying in an actual hotel for this gig.

As much as I liked Hope's tour bus, *La Esperanza*, I was ready for a real bed and a real shower. Maybe even a *bath*.

Hope was the first to go upstairs to bed. I'll admit, I wanted her to stay. Something about her presence, sitting there next to me, helped me feel safer. I imagined following her up to her cabin upfront for a nightcap but shook off the idea as fanciful and inappropriate.

Marcy, Babs, and Harlan filed up the stairs after her. This left me alone with Dribbler, who claimed he couldn't leave because Jasmine the cat sat on his lap. He seemed content to sit close with me on the couch, and I didn't mind his cozy company one bit. It was nice, just watching the garish neons, projection screens, and colorful lights of St. Louis slide past the window.

And the people! Gone were the face masks, suits, and dresses of bitter Gamma Earth, replaced in Delta by skin-tight Day-Glo clothing, big hair, and mirrored sunglasses. *Everyone* wore sunglasses at night.

"What's up with all the shades?" I asked Dribbler. "Do all the neon lights get to them?"

He laughed. "Naw. Those aren't *shades*, sweetie. They're *Specs*. VR glasses. Most of 'em can't live without 'em, like your phones back home. Except they wear 'em and see virtual reality layered over regular reality. Maps, name tagging, imaginary things, virtual costumes, that kind of thing."

"Huh. Doesn't that get in the way of seeing--" I gestured vaguely at the city streets. "—like, *everything*?"

Dribbler grinned and touched my hand with his fingertips. "You'd think. But some of 'em turn it all the way up, and never see any reality."

His touch sent a warm shiver up my arm. I decided to leave my hand where it was. "All the way up?"

He nodded, letting his hand settle on top of mine by unspoken agreement. "Yeah. They *only* see virtual. It's like walking around inside of a world-sized video game. Or so I hear."

I thought about that a bit, letting our hands stay together while I did. As I spoke, I extracted my hand and stroked the sleeping Jasmine. Her ears twitched, and her tail flipped once, but her eyes stayed shut. "Sounds risky. What if you go someplace that's not mapped out in virtual reality?"

He shrugged. "Dunno. I guess the things do some mapping for you? How much of *your* world isn't mapped out by Google?"

I bit my lip, then said, "Fair point. So, they have Google here?"

He shook his head. "Naw. They have a bunch of companies. Rover is the big one, I guess, they make the Specs. But another company does the software, and yet another built the VR net."

"Still seems a bit weird, seeing the world through VR glasses, but not too different from Beta."

Dribbler smiled. "I thought so, too. Delta Earth is fast-paced, high-energy. It's out to prove to you how smart and sexy it is. It's Electric Avenue in downtown Funkytown. They don't believe in 'chill' here, except when you're talking about subzero electric martinis at two in the morning. For shows here, Hope still plays some Blues, but she also busts out Disco, Hip-hop, and New Wave aesthetics to keep the Deltans awake."

I took all that in, watching the lights pass us by, thinning out as we left the city's center. I shifted my position on the couch such that I faced away from Dribbler, leaning against him, my head partly on the seat, and partly on his shoulder. When he didn't move away, I murmured, "Do you mind?"

His voice lowered to a hush. "Not at all, Jules. Now I have two cuties sleeping on me."

I must have answered him, probably to protest that I wasn't asleep, but it would have been a lie because I drifted off right about then.

I awoke sometime later to find the lights in the cabin had dimmed and Dribbler had gone. Jasmine perched along my side. My head lay upon a Dribbler's rolled-up hoodie. I shifted a little, looking around for him. The cat let me know with little claw pricks that she wanted me to stay right where I was. I gave in and fell back asleep for the rest of the trip.

The lights in the main cabin blazed to full brightness, and Marcy swept into the room, wearing an incandescent yellow dress with a repeating pattern of multi-colored birds all over it. "Rise and shine, Jules, we're at the hotel! You know you have your own bunk upstairs, right?"

"Well, Dribbler and I—" I began.

Marcy cut me off with a sly smile, saying, "I had a feeling about you two! Good for you!"

"But, um, I don't think that's how—"

She waved her hands between us, as though erasing a whiteboard. "No, no, I don't need to know details. Things get close here on *La Esperanza*, and it's good to keep some privacy!"

"Privacy? About what?" Babs appeared in the doorway from the aft galley, holding a steaming cup in one hand. "If there's any juicy gossip, I gotta know about it, come on!"

Marcy laughed. "I was just giving Jules here a hard time about—"

"About what?" Dribbler stumbled down the stairway in black jeans and a hot pink Madonna T-shirt. His hair was somehow perfect.

Babs kissed him on the cheek as they met at the bottom of the stairway. "Marcy was about to dish, Dribs!"

Marcy put her hands on her hips and grinned. "Well, speak of the devil and he shall appear! You sly dog, you!"

My face warmed a few thousand degrees. "It's not like—"

Dribbler's face suddenly matched his t-shirt much more closely. "Wasn't it, Jules? I mean, at least, *I* thought—"

I shook my head. "No, that's not what I meant. Last night was very cozy!"

Babs and Marcy mirrored each others' gleeful look. I thought they might jump up and down or burst out in a fit of giggles, but instead, they chorused, "Verrrry cozy!"

Just then, Hope swept into the room, swathed in shimmering teal gauze. She ruffled Dribbler's hair and slipped an arm around his waist. She sang, "Cozy? Who can help being cozy on this bus?"

Dribbler ran fingers through his hair to try to restore its former perfection. "Jules and I just watched the world go by together last night. They were very sweet."

Hope's muzzle drooped a little, as she now stared at his feet. "Oh Dribbler! How could you? I thought last night was *my* night! "

I stood up and straightened my long sweater. "What? I didn't know!" I stared daggers at Dribbler.

The cuddly drummer broke out into a wolfish grin. "I mean, we hadn't made up a schedule yet, but if you wanted Jules, you should have stuck around."

"Perhaps tonight, then," said Hope, fixing me with an inscrutable stare. She beckoned to me with one of her mitten-like hands.

"*What?*" I cried in confusion.

Harlan wandered in from the driver's cabin. "What seems to be the problem here? We goin' to the hotel, or ain't we?"

Marcy, Babs, Dribbler, and even Hope burst out into laughter.

My embarrassment heated up, and I made a beeline for the door, slapping the button to open the bus's hatch.

Dribbler caught my arm to stop me from storming out. "H-hey, Jules, we were just—"

I whirled on him. "Just what? Hazing the new person? Well, you got me. Very funny."

Hope began to sing, "Jules—"

I shook my head. "Sorry, I don't take teasing very well. Especially not after running away from my wedding to join the interdimensional circus. Forgive me for taking a little comfort in closeness with you all. I just started to feel at home, you know?"

Hope took a step to stand at Dribbler's side, brushing my other arm with her hand. "Lovely Jules," she sang, "no one is mocking you. We are all rather fond of you here, and we're glad you ran away with us."

Marcy looked from Babs to me and said, "Yeah, sorry about that. We just get excited when a new member of the crew hits it off with the rest of us. We *are* family here."

Babs took Marcy's hand and blew a lock of dark hair out of her eyes. "Yes. A rather *incestuous* family at times."

Marcy swatted at her. "Not like that!"

Babs fluttered her fingers between herself and Marcy. "Oooh, you *lie*, mama bear! Half the time, half of us sleep anywhere but our own cabins."

I wanted to get my chill back. I wanted to laugh it off. But adrenaline and disorientation wouldn't let me go of my mad. "Look, I just need some time to myself. Do I have a room to myself in the hotel?"

Marcy and Hope exchanged a look. Marcy said, "If you like. I *was* going to ask who you'd like to room with."

I shook my head. "At least for today and tonight, I want some space for just me. Okay?"

Everyone but Harlan nodded. Harlan said, "Y'all, as fun as this soap opera always is, could we get a move on so Zamboni can park the bus, and we can all get some brunch?"

Marcy distributed mirrored sunglasses. "These Specs are like wearable smartphones. Jules, I set up a pair for you. They'll act as your map, room key, credit card, and much more. I wouldn't put the opacity up past 50 percent until you know what you're doing, however."

"Opacity?"

Dribbler chimed in, "The VR level like we were talking about last night."

I nodded, not feeling like talking to him just now.

And with that, everyone descended the ramp into the cavernous orange-neon-lined parking garage. I trailed behind and discouraged attempts to pull me back into the fold. Signage everywhere welcomed us to the Horizon. As we ascended an escalator, I could tell that the Horizon was more than just a hotel; it was also a mall, a restaurant strip, and an entertainment complex. It reminded me of some of the hotel/casinos in Las Vegas, though I saw no evidence of gambling at first glance.

I put on the Specs Marcy had given me, and the world exploded with light and motion. People stood out against the background as though every one of them was lit perfectly. Some had elaborate clothing that seemed to be made of light, or even moving patterns. Most people had a caption floating over their heads with a name or handle of some kind to identify them. Marcy's handle said "Mardav84", while Harlan's read, "X-USDdiv31". Hope's said "Hopestour001", and Babs and Dribbler had -002 and -003. I peered upwards to find that mine just said "Jules".

Distracted, I stumbled as I found myself stepping into a fountain. Since I remained dry, I put out my hand and discovered the fountain to be entirely virtual. The droplets of water were scintillating pixels of light that even seemed to splash off of my brightly illuminated body.

The hotel lobby could have been one from back home on Beta Earth. Something upscale, dignified, and downtown for sure, not all sci-fi like the rest of the complex. The staff wore sharp uniform suits, and while none of them had Specs covering their eyes, I did notice a few had them sitting on top of their heads or hanging by straps around their necks. Marcy tipped up her glasses while checking us in, but others in the lobby didn't afford the staff this courtesy.

We rode up in the elevator together to the same floor. My room's door had a virtual green glow lining it in my Specs and a virtual skeleton key appeared in front of it. When I touched the key, it turned sideways, and the lock on my door clicked to green.

As I reached for the door handle, a hand touched my shoulder. I turned to see Hope watching me with her deep eyes, muzzle tipped slightly downwards. She sang, "Jules, are you all right?"

I looked away, drew a deep breath, and let it out. I met her eyes and nodded. "I will be. I just need some time alone. It's a lot to take in, and I have issues to sort out. I—I'm sorry for being such a poor sport. I just don't take teasing well sometimes."

She nodded and withdrew her hand. "All right. Take care of yourself, and we will be here when you need us. My door is always open."

I gave her a weak smile at that offer of comfort but pushed my way into my room without another word.

As I closed my door, Harlan called after me, "Show prep's at six, meet in the lobby! Don't be late!"

The room was small, but comfortable, everything in neutral tones in reality, but decorated with neon musical notes and instruments in virtual reality. I stripped down and took a wonderfully decadent hot shower, and I scrubbed myself from head to toe with the sandalwood-scented soap the hotel provided.

As I toweled off, I noticed my Specs flashing blue around the rims, so I put them on again. A picture of Dribbler, shaped like a stamp, floated in front of me. The caption said, "I'm sorry!". I grabbed it with my fingers and tossed it off to the side, where it shrank and sat as a tiny icon. I'd open it later when I felt more like company.

I paced the room, wearing the towel wrapped around me. I considered the plush bed but dismissed that idea. My head swirled with too many thoughts to rest right now. I crossed to the window and peered out from 12 stories up. I watched the flow of cars and pedestrians on the street below me. I found a pang of loneliness watching them, knowing that this was not my world. But despite not wanting the company of the only familiar people in Delta, I felt a need to get out of my little room to explore this place. I couldn't get lost, I had my Specs, so why not?

I found that my purple backpack had mysteriously appeared in the entryway to my room while I showered, so I rooted through it for something to wear. I hadn't packed anything in fluorescent colors to match this world's aesthetic, but I did have a knee-length magenta shift dress, which I paired with some deep purple tights and ballet flats. I considered my small clutch purse, which contained my Beta Earth IDs, credit cards, and paper money. I supposed that all of it would be worthless in this 'verse, except maybe for making conversation. Here in Delta, the Specs served the purpose of all that and much more.

I pushed away some dark thoughts and anxiety about venturing out alone and stepped out my door. To my relief, I failed to encounter anyone from the crew on my way to the elevator. I rode down to the lobby with a pack of excited swimsuit-clad preteens, who gave me and my outfit withering middle-school side-eyes, but otherwise ignored me.

As I stood in the lobby, undecided as to what to do, a virtual question mark appeared in front of me. I touched it, and it exploded into a dozen ads. Among them, restaurants, the pool, early shows, mani-pedis, and more. I considered some of these, then swiped them all into the virtual trash can in the corner of my vision.

Once my view cleared, a man stood in front of me.

Patrick, my ex-boyfriend.

"Oh, hey Jules! Fancy, uh, running into you here!" he stammered out.

I crossed my arms. "Uh-huh. Just by chance. A world or two away, and you *happen* to be in the lobby of the Delta Earth Chicago Horizon hotel, where I *happen* to be staying. Ain't serendipity a funny thing?"

He wrung his hands, twisting the untucked plaid buttoned shirt he wore in his fingers. "Yeah, I know. I had to see you. So, I looked up where Hope's Tour was scheduled and caught up with you here."

I took a breath and closed the distance and hugged him tightly. I took a step back and looked up into his face. "Patrick, I've only been gone a couple of days. Why do you need to see me already?"

"It's Sam, Jules. We have to talk about Sam."

My heart sank like a rock, but I let him take me by the hand to lead me away.

I sat, facing my ex-boyfriend across the table, the remaining half of a steaming Chicago deep-dish pizza between us. "Patrick, I know what I did was shitty. Running away like that, leaving her at the altar—Did you *have* to travel between worlds and track me down, just to tell me what I already know? I mean, hello, I ran away for a reason."

He carved out two more thick slices of the pie and placed them on plates in front of each of us. "No, I didn't have to. Sam's a wreck, though, and her dad's apoplectic. They've been screaming at me for explanations, demanding I tell them where you went. *Why* you left."

My mind wandered back to the day I left. Back to the hour beforehand. Lost in thought, I stared at the massive slice of pizza in front of me, to avoid meeting Patrick's eyes. "Look, it wasn't just cold feet. It was about respecting myself."

Maybe it was because he had a mouth full of pizza, but for once, Patrick just listened to me.

I sighed. "On the day of the wedding, while I was getting ready, just before the cat showed up, I heard William's voice in the hallway. *Mister* Edgewood was having a fit. He said—he said some ugly things. Patrick, I admit it. I *did* have some doubts about getting married to Sam. You know I loved her, and she loved me. But come on. She's from money, the daughter of a tycoon and a socialite. I'm a bartender, a stagehand, an Uber driver. I'm non-binary and queer. How do I even fit into their upper crust world?"

Patrick touched my hand and said, "Sam didn't care about any of that. She loved *you*, blue hair, they-them pronouns, and all!"

I shook my head, but let his hand lay across my balled-up fist. "Patrick, her dad said something to Sam that tore it for me. They were out in the hallway. I don't think they knew I was in my dressing room at the time. No way Sam would have chanced us seeing each other before the ceremony. Anyway, my father-in-law to be, he said, 'I don't care if my daughter is marrying a man or a woman, but for God's sake, I wish it would make up its mind which it is!'."

Patrick gasped. "Shit. He really called you 'it'?"

I looked up at him and nodded. "You know I don't care about pronouns all that much." I waved a hand back and forth. "He, she, they, it's all the same to me. I don't care about that. Gender doesn't apply to me. But 'it'? That's dehumanizing!"

"Yeah, I get that. Crappy of the old guy to say something like that. But couldn't you have hashed that out with him after the wedding?"

"It wasn't only that, Patrick," I sighed. "And it wasn't just my fears about not being 'good enough' for her family, either. No, sweetie, the worst part was Sam. She didn't defend me. All she said was, 'well, Jules is just *different*, daddy.' She could have told him not to expect me to be a man or a woman for him, she could have been upset at him calling me 'it'. But she didn't, and she wasn't. She took the easy route of trying to placate him, on our wedding day. And my future rolled out before me, knowing my partner wouldn't back me up. I just can't be with someone who won't stand up for me, and I can't be a part of a family that has no respect for me. Does that make sense?"

He shrugged. "So, when a cat came along and stole the ring, you took that as your ticket out?"

The room blurred, and I wiped at my eyes. "I didn't know what else to do! Maybe I should have told Sam, but you know her. She'd have insisted we go through with it and talk about it later. It was a coward's way out, but it was the only way out."

"Hey, hey, it's okay! I'm on your side, Jules! I'm always on your side. You know that."

I met his eyes. "I know you are. And it's not really about 'sides' anyway. It's about respect and compatibility."

He nodded. "So, um, how's the new gig going?"

I smiled and shrugged. "They're great people. Hope herself is dazzling, alien, kind, and beautiful. I fit in with the crew surprisingly well."

Maybe even too *well?*

He looked around us. "So, where are they, then? I'd love to meet them."

I bit my lip and cast my eyes downward. "I—well, as nice as they've been, it's still an adjustment, and you know me, I need my alone time. *Me* time."

Though I couldn't see his gaze, I knew Patrick stared at me critically. "Uh-huh. You do. But that's not the whole story. I didn't get a ticket to another world just to be fed bullshit by my favorite ex, Jules. Come on, don't you trust me?"

Damn him! He knows me too well! Feelings from earlier this morning still tangled up in my heart, I did *not* want to talk it out with my ex right this moment. But knowing Patrick, he'd poke at me and pick at it and leave me a mess if I let him. I needed some air, and I needed to change the subject.

I met his eyes as I wadded up my napkin and stood. "I have to go to the restroom. I'll be back in a minute."

"Hey, Jules—" he began.

I turned and strode away from him toward the facilities before he could stop me.

As I approached the restrooms, I was forced into an annoying choice. There was only a "men's" room and a "women's" room. *Of course!* So, after the treatment I'd had in Gamma, and given that I wore a dress, and I hadn't seen any men in skirts or dresses so far, I chose the women's room, for my safety.

The restroom turned out to be empty, to my relief. I took care of some biological business and then proceeded to wash my hands and face. As I dried my face with paper towels and considered whether I wanted to apply some makeup, the strangest thing happened.

I saw two of me in the mirror, one wearing different clothing than me, a deep purple jumpsuit that gathered at the wrists and ankles and plunged at the neckline.

The other Jules wore their Specs up on top of their head. They smiled at me with lips that matched their freshly dyed blue hair. Their haircut matched mine exactly.

I whirled to face them. "What? How did you—"

They held a finger to their lips and said, "Keep it low and hold your questions, we don't have much time. We need to switch clothes and Specs, and we have to do it in the next minute or so, or they'll know I'm up to something."

I mean, if another you told *you* something, would you believe them?

I said, "Why should I do that? I don't even know you."

They smiled a smile I'd only seen on me in candid photos. "Of course you do. I'm you, or at least the next best thing. And if you can't trust yourself, who can you trust? Look, we have no time, and I want you to see something, but you can only see it if they think I'm you."

I crossed my arms in front of me. "Still not selling it, not even with that pretty face."

They chuckled. "Okay, let's put it this way. Know how people keep attacking Hope's Tour? Want to know why?"

I nodded. "As it happens, another one of me—of us —was involved in one of those attacks. So, tell me what you know, right now."

They scowled and shook their head. "No. You have to see it to understand. You have to be *me* for an hour or so. Hope's in terrible danger, and so is her crew. You know that. You have to know more if you want to keep them all safe."

I took in a deep breath and let it out in a gust. "Do you know anything about that other me, from Achse?".

Their eyebrows bunched up together. "A Jules from Achse? No, I don't know anything about them."

Ah. They said, 'them', not 'her'. A good sign, unless this Jules was a much better actor than I am. I'd like to think I could tell if another me was lying to me if we're essentially the same person at some level.

I considered. "Patrick would know something's up."

The other Jules grinned. "Patrick won't know I'm not you. I've got a Patrick of my own. He's one of my spouses. Let's say I know him pretty well. Come on, just give me an hour. What have you got to lose? If it doesn't work out, just go back to Hope's Tour and get a new pair of Specs."

On the one hand, it did *not* seem like a good choice to do as this other me asked. The last me I'd encountered chased my friends around in a walking war machine, firing bolts of energy at them. I had no reason whatsoever to trust them.

On the other, well, something needed to be done about the attacks. And if I could get some information about what lay behind them, maybe I could help stop them from happening. Or help keep my new friends safe.

I sighed and put my Specs on the counter. "Fine. It'll be an adventure. Another adventure. But if there's a chance of protecting Hope, I'll take it." They gave me a big grin, and I started to wiggle my way out of my magenta dress.

In moments, we wore each other's clothing and Specs. The jumpsuit felt as light and breezy as parachute cloth but didn't cling to my skin. My double offered a hand, and I shook it. It was the strangest sensation, and to be honest, the room spun around me a little as we did this.

"Now, I'm going to lead Patrick off. You stay in here another couple of minutes, then follow the map on your Specs to what I need you to see."

I watched them slip out of the restroom without another word.

A minute or so after the other Jules left, a woman and her daughter entered the restroom, finding me just standing there, staring at the door.

"Are you all right?" asked the woman, lifting her Specs to peer at me with concern. Her daughter looked up at me with wide eyes.

"I—I think so."

The little girl said, "You look like you've seen a ghost!"

I laughed. "Maybe I have. Thanks for your concern, but I have to go."

I left the restroom and peered in the direction I'd come, but neither Patrick nor my double were anywhere in sight. I pulled my Specs down over my eyes and found that my twin had a far richer virtual world than I had. The virtual handle above me said, 'J. Martin'. In addition to the mall complex's virtual decorations, one corner of my vision contained a thumbnail map with a route traced in yellow upon it. On the ground in front of me, a matching yellow line ran from my feet, down the corridor, and around a corner.

I laughed out loud.

"Follow the Yellow Brick Road," I sang to myself, as I took a breath and proceeded on down the glowing line towards my unknown destination.

Chapter 12 – Dead Shrimp Blues

The yellow line in my twin's virtual reality Specs took me out of the massive Horizon hotel complex and out onto the street. With my Specs on, the scene overwhelmed my senses. The people in the bustling crowd on the sidewalks each wore handles floating over their heads, many with virtual avatars superimposed over their clothing. The cars that passed had their appearance augmented with fancy styles, racecar numbering, neon piping, and even animated advertisements in some cases. The buildings seemed to be covered in gargantuan television screens, flashing ads and logos, and ten-story smiling faces in such disharmony, my head swam, and I became dizzy. I found the control for opacity, and turned it down to twenty percent, and learned to keep my eyes cast downward to avoid becoming confused and overwhelmed.

I marveled at the sheer scale of everything. Here in the heart of the city, it seemed the base of every building took up a full block or even several blocks. Most of the buildings had enclosed connecting catwalks that crossed streets to other buildings. It seemed like Delta Earth Chicagoans could live entirely indoors if they chose to.

And I could see why they might want to. The fall weather back home in Beta had been chilly, it had been frosty in Gamma, but here in late morning Delta, I began to sweat in the sweltering air. I understood better why people wore skimpier clothing here, out of necessity.

As a little experiment, I removed my Specs to look at the raw world around me. Without them, colors faded to drab, cars and buildings showed their dirt and weathering, and the people on the streets lost much of their exotic glamor. The sky lost its blue, replaced by a yellowish layer of smog halfway up the tallest buildings. I watched in amusement as the foot traffic bent around a space that had contained a neon tree in virtual space. I considered standing in that spot for a respite from the chaos but felt the urgency of my quest tug at me.

I replaced my Specs and resumed following the yellow line, which overlaid the streets like full-scale GPS. After a couple of long blocks, the line bent and led into an elevated train station. Like everything else, the shabby station had a space-age sheen in virtual reality. I began to understand the appeal of turning the opacity all the way up, as Patrick had suggested last night.

Had that only been last night? Waking up in a new world, wandering away from my new companions, seeing Patrick, and meeting my doppelganger all in a few hours made it seem like days ago.

The yellow line led to a square with "Millennium Park" inside it. A train arrived, so I hopped on, and grabbed a vertical rail. I watched the electronic sign, which had a virtual counterpart that followed my vision. People on the packed train car ignored one another, staring straight ahead into their Specs. Some doodled or typed in midair, some swiped in front of them as though turning pages in a large book.

After half a dozen stops, a voice announced the Millennium Park station. I exited to the train platform and let the current of people sweep me along the yellow line. A Metra train station stood on one side of the street, but the yellow line led across from it, into the pyramid-like Delta Earth Arch Authority building. The glass walls of the great ground-level hangar-like space afforded a somewhat clear view of the massive Arch and numerous trucks and transports inside.

Though I followed the line, my stomach tightened, not knowing what I might be getting myself into. I had no desire whatsoever to pass into fascist Achse, especially not alone. I stood outside the glass doors to the Arch station, annoying people for whom I'd become an obstacle. I gathered my courage and followed the virtual path inside.

My guiding line swept past the registration and ticketing counters, to a wide bank of escalators in the far distance. As I passed the second Una Mas Coffee kiosk on my way to the escalators, a startlingly familiar voice called out to me.

"Jules!" came the voice of my ex-fiancée, Samantha. "Jules, baby, slow down!"

Anxiety rose in me. I had no nerve for a confrontation just now. Then, realization dawned on me. This wasn't the Sam I left at the altar. This was Delta Sam, about whom I knew very little. Anxiety escalated to panic, and I debated just running for it.

Her hand touched my shoulder and I stopped and turned to face her.

My heart melted at the face smiling up at me. With no other ideas, I just blurted out, "Hey, Sam. Fancy meeting you here?" She wore black culottes over bright red tights, her top covered by a white silk short-sleeved blouse. I'd never seen her strawberry blonde hair cut that short in an undercut before. My Sam wouldn't have dreamed of anything that wild.

She stood on tiptoe and kissed me on the lips. She wrinkled her nose, freckles gathering in a pretty constellation across her face just under her Specs. "Silly! Is that any way to greet your wife! We both work here, why wouldn't you see me? Missed you at the weekly status meeting an hour ago. Everything okay?"

Wife? So, Delta me had gone through with it. And we worked together, at the Arch Authority?

I nodded, heart racing as I struggled to make conversation. "Sorry about that, I got caught up with Patrick at brunch, then ran into an old friend. I hope I won't be in too much trouble."

She laughed. "Oh yeah, like you *ever* get in trouble. I swear you can do no wrong here. I think maybe it comes with your clearance level. I know if *I* missed the status meeting, Miz Davenport wouldn't let me hear the end of it for days!"

"Miz Davenport?" I exclaimed, caught off guard. I tried to cover for it by saying, "Oh, don't worry about Marcy. She's all bark and no bite."

Delta Sam studied me for a long, uncomfortable moment. "You think so? Huh."

I held up my hands. "Hey, don't tell her I said so, okay, or maybe she'll try to prove me wrong!"

She laughed, and I forced a laugh along with her.

Before she could launch into another difficult line of conversation, I held up a finger. "As late as I am, I'd better get going. No time for Una Mas today!"

She shrugged and handed me a hot paper cup. "Who's always looking out for you? Who's your favorite wife?" She fluttered her eyelashes and watched my face with great interest.

A lump of guilt weighed heavy in my stomach, and I doubted the coffee would help wash it away. I sipped at the piping hot liquid. "Mocha, my favorite! Okay, *you're* my favorite."

She grinned and patted my bottom affectionately. "I knew it! Don't worry, I won't tell Patrick that either!"

Oh. The other Jules *had* said that Patrick was "one of his spouses". Plural.

I risked a joke. "I can't imagine how I'd get along without either of you. Now, I have to go, okay?"

She pouted at me and hooked a dainty little hand around my elbow. "Nope! You can't ditch me that easily. I'm in meetings the rest of the day, so I'm at *least* going to walk you up to your office!"

The yellow line led down an escalator, Sam led me upwards, several floors, to a labyrinth of partitioned cubicles. Without Specs, each cube had blank gray carpeting for walls, unadorned. But with Specs on, each had been plastered with posters, clocks, photos, and even animated virtual pets. No workstation sat at each, only a chair. No need for a monitor or keyboard when one had Specs, I supposed.

As we walked, the Specs tried to reroute me back downward, but I resisted its nagging, to keep up appearances with Sam. I hid behind the mocha and let her natter on about the very corporate details of the day ahead of her, responding with "uh-huh" and "oh!" and "that's terrible!" at what seemed like the appropriate points.

As we arrived at a cubicle that looked pretty much like all the others, she said, "Here's your stop, baby. Now give me some sugar!"

She flipped up her Specs, and I saw her eyes clearly for the first time. Could I tell the difference between my Sam and this parallel Sam in those sparkling sea-green eyes? I stepped toward her, uncertain whether I had an answer to that question, but she stopped me with the palm of her hand flat against my chest.

She pretended to scold me. "Rude! Specs up, darling! I don't make the rules, I just enforce them!"

I slid the VR glasses up on top of my head and waited.

"Much better!" she proclaimed and pulled me in for a tight hug and intimate kiss.

That lump in my stomach fluttered a bit, then sank even heavier into my gut, as the thought came to me, "did I make a mistake leaving my Sam?"

And then, with a wave, Sam bounced off, lost to view in Cubeville.

I sat down at my desk for a moment, partly to blend in, and partly to catch my breath and get my bearings. The other Jules had decorated the cube's walls with show posters from rock concerts, theatrical productions, and moving photos of Sam and Patrick, alone or various combinations with and without Jules. A virtual screen appeared in front of me on the desk.

My Specs still overlaid a yellow path down the corridor, now leading to a bank of elevators. I pinched the map in to show me where it led down to a basement corridor to an area labeled "Generator" and a specific lab titled, "Coral [classified]". The line ended there in an X. I supposed X marked the spot Delta Jules wanted me to see for myself.

I raised my hands, and a ghostly keyboard formed under them. I tapped out "What is Coral?" and was met with "no entries found". I clicked in the air on the "Coral [classified]" label and the word "classified" turned red and enlarged. A bubble popped up next to it which read, "That information is not available via Specs. Please use a secure terminal for access."

I had no idea where a secure terminal might be, so I took a deep breath, stood up, and began to follow the line once more.

I struggled against the urge to hold my breath as I made my way through the winding paths between cubes on my way to the elevator. My random encounter with Sam had gone as well as it possibly could, but I had no confidence in my ability to bluff the next co-worker.

I drew in a deep breath and let it out in a relieved sigh as I made it to the elevator lobby and pressed the "down" button.

As the elevator in front of me opened, a tall, mustached man stepped out and pointed at me. "Jules! I have *got* to get with you about the latest from Achse!"

I waved him off. "Later, sorry, I'm late for a meeting as it is!"

He shot me with a finger-gun and said, "gotcha! I'll put something on your calendar!"

I dodged around him and into the elevator car. The SB light glowed yellow in my Specs, so I pressed it. I pressed a few more times in hopes of getting the elevator doors to shut before anyone else could join me.

One floor down, the car stopped, and let in a lithe Latina woman, cool as could be behind her Specs. The tag over her head said, "Bárbara, Marketing".

I decided to take a chance. "Hey, Babs! How's it going?"

She turned and regarded me like I was a bug that had landed on her lunch plate. "Yes?" she glanced up at the handle floating above my head. "Do I know you, hmmm, 'J. Martin'?"

I frowned, not sure what to say next.

In the space my indecision left, something dawned on her face and she smiled. "Oh! You're *Jules* Martin! I'm so sorry not to have realized! You have me at the disadvantage, Mx Martin! I didn't know you knew who I am!"

I played it as cool as I could. I nodded. "Your name has come up in meetings. Let's get lunch sometime?"

The elevator stopped at the ground floor level. She flashed me a nervous smile and said, "Sure! I'd be honored! I'll send you an interoffice message!" Without waiting for a reply from me, she dashed out into the lobby, and the doors shut behind her.

I hoped this jumpsuit didn't show sweat stains, because, by this time, I was quite damp from being at red alert through the uncomfortable encounters.

Alone, at last, I rode the next few floors down to the sub-basement level and followed the yellow line down a long, breezy corridor, lit with old buzzing fluorescent tubes at intervals. The walls had signs painted, with foot-high letters. The signs pointed back the way I came, saying "ELEVATORS, MAIN COMPLEX" and forward with "ARCH, GENERATOR".

A few people passed me going the other way, and they touched fingers to their specs, like one might tip a hat. I returned the gesture.

As I approached the far end of the subterranean corridor, the walls vibrated with a low thrumming that didn't help my nerves one bit. I soon found myself standing in front of the door that contained the X at the end of my journey.

What would I find inside? I imagined a room full of photos, news clippings, and strings to connect them in an intricate web, all tracking Hope's location and planned appearances. Or maybe a control center, with banks of monitors and terminals, live footage of each of my new friends showing on each.

Would the person behind the attacks be sitting in the middle of the room, where the X marked the spot? Should I have come armed? The other Jules hadn't said so, but maybe I'd been too gullible, trusting them like that. Maybe it was an elaborate trap, meant to draw me away from Hope and her crew, to capture me and wring information out of me.

I could still turn around and go back. I could rejoin my crew and tell Hope what little I'd learned so far. Maybe Harlan could get some information out of Delta Jules' Specs, so I wouldn't have to put myself in further danger.

Or maybe, the Specs would lead a would-be killer right back to Hope.

I drew in a breath and opened the door.

Inside the room marked Coral, I found a giant cylindrical tank, reminding me of antique iron lungs I'd seen in books. Windows along one side showed it to be mostly full of water, lit with a soft pink glow. There was a printed label under the window on one end, which said, "Coral".

Also, inside the tank, floated a body.

Not just *any* body, but a dolphin-like one. A dolphin-like body with limbs and head and muzzle very much like Hope's. A Tristellian! Except, this one was naked, with subtle differences in coloration and shape. This body also had wires attached to bands around their wrists, ankles, and neck. The wires led off to a bundle that left the tank from the top and fed into what looked like a cabinet-sized computer. A single monitor and terminal sat on a desk next to the computer, away from the tank.

I peered in at the body and found one of the occupant's eyes staring out at me glassily.

I tapped on the glass, and called out, "Hello, are you Coral?"

The eye blinked twice. The body let out a series of shrill squeaks and clicks.

My Specs translated for me, providing the reply in subtitles.

"Help me," said Coral. "Please, help me!"

Chapter 13 – Sweet Home Chicago

I stared at the humanoid cetacean in the tank, too stunned to do anything. Now that I looked closer, gauzy dead tissue wreathed the poor creature's skin from nose to tail. Compared with Hope, Coral appeared gaunt and withered. Sickly. I didn't know what to say, so I blurted out, "Help you? Are you hurt?"

The Tristellian repeated the high-pitched whistle of distress, and my Specs dutifully translated, "Help me!"

A virtual button appeared before me. "Translate Yes/No?" I clicked the "yes" and said, "How can I help you?"

An external speaker on my Specs let out a burst of clicks and squeals, to which Coral responded similarly. "Set me free!"

I examined my options. I couldn't just leave this being—this *person*—in this tiny prison. I found latches along the sides of the tank and began undoing them one at a time. "Who did this to you?"

The Specs read me Coral's reply. "You did. The Jules from here."

I stopped and stared Coral in the eyes. "How do you know I'm not from here?"

Coral squeaked and clicked. "No time to tell. I can *feel* the difference. You vibrate differently than this world. You don't belong here. I do not either."

I continued undoing the latches, keeping one eye on the attached computer equipment for signs that might tell me whether it might sound an alarm. "Why did the other me put you in there?"

Coral replied, "To keep the Arch connected."

"What? I don't get what you mean?" I undid the last latch and pushed upward on handles on the top half of the cylinder. With a bit of effort, it swung open like a clamshell. The stink of rot and seawater rolled out, overpowering my senses. I couldn't help but let out a groan at the stench.

A slimy, mitten-like hand grasped my forearm and kept me from backing away. I fought my instinct to strike at the creature to free myself, as I realized Coral needed my help to get out of the tank.

Coral thrashed in the half-cylinder and made strangled gurgling noises. The Specs failed to translate anything but, "—help—".

I grasped Coral's slick arm with my other hand and helped hoist them out of the tank. It was a struggle, between the disgusting slime covering their body and their weakened condition, but after a short while, we sat upon swampy puddles on the floor.

"Thank you," said Coral, breathing hard. They pulled at the bands, still connected to wires, freeing themselves from the electronics.

Red indicator lights winked on one after another on the nearby console.

"Sure. I'm not sure where we go from here, though. You're pretty conspicuous. What did you mean about the Arch?"

Coral looked at me and said, "Without one of us, the Arch can not maintain its path. It is my mind that has kept this pathway open."

A red envelope flashed in the corner of my augmented vision. The Specs told me I had an incoming message. "I think we're in trouble. Seems like the locals know you're not hooked up anymore."

Coral nodded and let out a sad whistle. "Certainly, my unwilling service will be missed immediately."

I leaped to my feet and began to search the little lab room. I threw a lab coat at Coral. "Get dressed, we have to move."

In a locker bearing my name, that opened to my touch, I found a pair of non-functioning Specs, some paper money in a clip, an opaque yellow scarf, and galoshes. The latter were a terrible fit for Coral, but we managed to stuff their webbed feet inside. Specs covered alien eyes, scarf wrapped around their head, and hid their cetacean muzzle. After I admonished them to keep their tail under the long lab coat, they almost passed for an awkwardly shaped human.

"I'm sorry to have to say this, but there's nothing I can do to hide your smell. They kept you in terrible conditions."

"Inhuman," said Coral.

"Agreed. I can't believe any version of myself could do this," I said, setting a route on my Specs' map, back to the hotel and the tour bus.

"Jules was kindest. After a time, they treated me as a person. A person who is a prisoner, but a person. They sent you, yes?"

I nodded. "They said they wanted me to see something for myself and sent me here."

"Then this is their doing, as are these coverings. I am thankful. Let us go while we can."

I held Coral back with one hand while I opened the door and looked out into the hallway. No red alert lights, no honking klaxons. Just a few other people, walking with purpose, up and down the long corridor. The yellow line in my Specs led back towards the elevators. We didn't dare take that route. I felt sure others would be on their way from that direction by now.

I pulled Coral out into the corridor and shut the door behind us. "Try to keep your distance from other people, we don't need anyone to examine you up close."

Coral nodded.

We got some funny looks from the people we passed, likely due to Coral's aroma of abuse. My stomach tightened, hoping no one would stop us. I urged Coral to walk faster, but the mismatch between the shape of their feet and the oversized galoshes forced them to maintain a ponderous gait.

All the while, the path back to safety pointed behind us. The thrumming of the Arch generators grew ever louder as we progressed.

We reached a T intersection, with a set of escalators on either side. A sign told me that one led to the generators, the other to the Arch Plaza.

Coral bowed their head and clutched it in their hands. "The Arch field is right above us, I can not bear to stay here, Jules."

A woman stopped in her tracks at the sound of Coral's whistles and clicks. She lifted her Specs and looked directly at us. She wrinkled her nose and said, "Did you fall in the lake or something?"

I had to think fast. I pulled off my Specs, took two steps toward her, and glared. "That's pretty rude! My friend is one of the leading marine biologists at Shedd!"

She took a step back and waved her Specs around as though to erase what she'd said. "Oh! I'm sorry! I'll get out of your way!"

I escorted Coral around her and up the Arch Plaza escalator without another word, relieved that my bluff had worked.

As our heads rose above the plaza's floor level, I almost cheered out loud as I saw something that might help us.

Rain.

The skies had opened up, and rain poured down the glass walls of the plaza, as though we stood underwater. The rain would mask Coral's smell, and I doubted anyone would look at us as closely as they hurried through the bad weather.

As we reached the top, my heart nearly stopped as I heard a voice. "Going somewhere, sweet cheeks?"

I whirled to face my ex-boyfriend, who now wore an Arch Authority Security uniform, his face grim and serious. "Patrick! What—"

"Shut up, Jules. Hand over those Specs."

"But—"

"Do it! Right now!" I'd never heard such a fierce tone out of him before. I guessed by the uniform that this wasn't *my* Patrick, but the Delta version.

I debated just running for it, but Coral couldn't run, and I wasn't abandoning them. I thought about bluffing him but knew Patrick was smarter than that. He had us, and there was nothing for me to do but cooperate. I handed over my Specs.

Patrick dropped the Specs to the ground and crushed them under his boot. "It was a shame your Specs got damaged in the struggle before you escaped," he said, eyes unreadable behind his own VR glasses.

Oh!

I got the idea. "Gotcha. But why—"

His tone softened. "Go, Jules. You're not gonna have much of a chance as it is. Don't stand around here talking to me. Just go, as quickly as you can."

I nodded and turned to grab Coral's arm, guiding them out into the Arch plaza. To my surprise, the area under the arch still contained the rippling mirror-like surface of the interdimensional portal. However, as we made our way out into the plaza, a Humvee-like transport drove into the portal—but was thrown back as sparks exploded from the point of contact.

Coral let out a stream of whistles and clicks. I wished I still had my Specs to translate, but Coral made the message clear by pointing at the gate. Then the Tristellian changed direction, and I was dragged along by their larger mass and determination.

"Wait, no, we can't!" I cried, trying to divert the upright cetacean towards the plaza's bank of exit doors. I doubted they'd understand, but I continued. "Didn't you see what happened? We're going to get caught, and you'll end up back in the tank!"

Shouts came from the other side of the Arch, and I spied a group of uniformed Arch Authority guards rushing towards us, brandishing metal batons. Electric sparks danced on the heads of some of the batons, and I didn't want to find out what it felt like to be tazed by those things.

Coral doubled their efforts and I had to let go of their arm. They kicked off the ill-fitting boots and began to move at a faster pace directly towards the shimmering wall of energy. I called after them, but Coral ignored me.

Glancing behind me, the half dozen guards closed in even faster, feet pounding on the concrete plaza floor. Other pedestrians scattered to get out of their path, yelling in confusion and irritation. The lead guard bellowed, "STOP! Surrender the Arch Authority's property immediately and you will not be harmed!"

As Coral neared the portal's surface, I caught up. I didn't dare look back, but from the sounds of running feet, the guards couldn't be more than a few seconds behind me. I grabbed Coral's shoulder and yelled, "Don't do this! We'll find another way!"

Coral shook me off and threw themself ahead, into the gate. They vanished into the mirrored surface.

The mirror revealed that the guards were right behind me.

I had a choice, and I had only an instant to make it. Stop and be apprehended or plunge on ahead to wherever Coral had gone. Coral hadn't burst into sparks or bounced back, so perhaps they'd gone on to fascist Achse somehow. Would going there with a fugitive alien from another world be a better fate than being caught by Delta Arch Authority goons? Did I want to be separated from Hope's Tour?

I heard a shout, then electricity crackled behind me, and my left leg went numb.

I decided that if Coral could go through once, they could go back through, so I held my breath and plunged into the mirrored surface.

And then, I fell in darkness. Or maybe I floated since I fell for an indeterminate amount of time. Maybe it was a few seconds, maybe it was a few minutes. I had no concept of where I was, or how long it took, but in a way, it was as though I didn't exist. Or maybe the rest of the world didn't?

And then, I landed, flat on my stomach, splayed out on a hard, smooth, cold concrete floor. The world spun crazily around me, and I fought my way to my feet, despite only the haziest notion of which way "up" was, and pins and needles in my left foot and calf.

People milling around me seemed not to notice me. Several vehicles stood stopped at the edge of the mirrored wall of energy behind me.

Where was I? The people wore tight neons and outrageous patterns. More telling, every one of them wore Specs. *Am I still in Delta? Then where are the guards? Why isn't it raining outside? Where is Coral?*

The answers to my questions would have to wait. I hobbled my way away from the portal, towards the glass wall opposite the Arch, and its row of doors. With every step, the hairs on the back of my neck prickled, expecting another shock from a baton, perhaps disabling me for capture this time. With every step, the pins and needles grew angrier and more pointed as feeling began to return to my foot and leg.

But with every step, I drew closer to the exit doors and freedom. As I reached the middle of the plaza, I realized the signs over the exits read, "Lake", which was not the street I'd come in on. *This is the other side of the Arch! I didn't go through to another dimension, I just passed through to the other side in Delta!*

Which meant that I'd left my pursuers on the other side of a wide wall. But this also meant that I still had pursuers, at least if they realized it.

As I reached the exits, I heard raised voices arguing back in the plaza, back towards the Arch. It took everything in me not to test my prickly-numb foot by breaking out into a run. If I ran, they'd see the movement and spot me for sure.

I opened the door and let a man in an electric blue jumpsuit through ahead of me. He touched his Specs in thanks, and I followed behind him, handing the open door off to an older woman in a stiff grey uniform.

Something seemed off about the city to me, and again I questioned whether this was Delta Earth. But the more I looked around me at the city and its people, the more convinced I became that I hadn't traveled to another 'verse.

The door shut on the commotion going on behind me, and I still refused to look back. I decided to follow the guy in the electric blue jumpsuit until I had a better plan. He turned left, crossed the street, and then left again. I needed to change clothes, and maybe get a hat to cover my blue hair. I ducked into a revolving door to get off the street and found myself inside another massive indoor complex, shops, and businesses stretching off into the neon-lit distance. I spied three separate clothing stores from the entrance, and though the first two tempted me with exotic Deltan styles, I slipped into an athletic wear shop.

I traded my pretty deep purple jumpsuit for some black leggings and a baggy red sweatshirt bearing the face of an angry bull. I bought these, along with a black stocking cap with another bull logo. I paid for the clothes with some of the paper money. I changed in the store before leaving and tossed the rolled-up jumpsuit in a trash can out in the food court.

Sitting on a bench near a fountain, I stopped awhile to catch my breath and figure out my next move. I had no Specs, and therefore no identification, or map, and only what was left of the paper money my twin had left me. At the same time, I no longer had a built-in tracking device and judging from the way I'd had to dodge out of the way of so many people in this mall, I was virtually invisible to those who turned up the opacity on their Specs too high.

I thought about Coral, wearing that ridiculous attempt at a disguise we'd tried to pass off, stumbling into Achse, probably to be captured by their Arch Authority. Why had they done that? For that matter, how long a walk would that be for them, through the non-space-time between portals? We drove through in comfort inside of Hope's bus, *La Esperanza.* But on foot? What would that even be like? Could Coral get lost? Did they know something I didn't?

Given how very little I understood about travel between 'verses, the latter seemed most likely. After all, the Tristellians had traveled between the dimensions in verseships, which had brought Hope, and probably Coral, to the various Earths connected by the Arches.

For Coral's sake, I hope they knew more than I did, and had a plan. They were beyond my help now, so all that remained was for me to help myself. What should I do now? The first order of business seemed to be to get away from the Arch Authority. I needed to get back to the Horizon and Hope's crew. Harlan had said to meet at six in the lobby for show prep. By now, it had to be about lunchtime, didn't it?

I got up from the bench and wandered my way towards an exit. Having Specs meant always knowing where you were, and what time it was. Without them, I had to manage the old-fashioned way, in a world where virtually no one did that. It took finding an electronics store to find an actual clock anywhere.

Inside the Rad Shack, I didn't believe the first clock I found, because if it read true, it was already after 6 pm. Since there's no way my travels had taken more than a couple of hours, it simply couldn't be right. I checked clock after clock. Every clock in the store read the same thing, within a second of each other; somehow, they told me it was 7:03

pm. I asked the salesperson if there could be anything wrong with them; maybe they'd all been set to Greenwich Mean Time for some reason?

She looked at me with bunched-up eyebrows. "It's really that late. Maybe you had too many at lunch?" She mimed drinking from a bottle and smiled.

I hurried out of the store and out of the complex onto Michigan Avenue. Sure enough, the rays of the sun cut long orange swaths across the city streets, peeking through buildings to the west.

Chapter 14 – Little Queen of Spades

I used the last of my folding money to buy a ticket to my own show, which was already underway. After finding an advertisement for Hope's Tour concert time and location, I'd made my way across the city on the El and on foot. My ticket was for a seat far back in the balcony of the old Harmony theater. I knew the analog of the place back home in my home 'verse, very little seemed changed, other than the name and some choices in renovation. This one had opted for more spartan deco, where back home, the owners had gone to the expense of restoring the beautiful turn of the 20th-century architectural adornments. I guessed that Deltans embellished with virtual frills, rather than tangible ones.

Without Specs, I had no idea what everyone else saw, but the place still had a quiet majesty about it, wearing the weight of over a century of musical and theatrical shows like a tattered but royal robe.

As I entered, Hope's beautiful voice lifted my spirits as she trilled Billie Holliday's "Let's Call the Whole Thing Off". Babs did the counterpoint of "toe-MAH-toe" to Hope's "toe-MAY-toe," and I couldn't help the big grin that spread across my face.

I was *home*.

I made my way to my seat, just to survey the situation. Casually dressed Deltans sparsely occupied the back rows of the balcony, each wearing a pair of Specs. It occurred to me that a distant seat like this might not be as much of an impediment to someone with a pair of the ubiquitous virtual reality glasses, since the scene could likely be magnified, or augmented through a feed from closer cameras.

On stage, Babs switched to an electric guitar and began a throbbing, driving baseline. Hope lowered her voice to a husky Janis Joplin level, grinding out Led Zeppelin's "Whole Lotta Love" like she was coming on to every last person in the Harmony theater.

I might have broken out in a sweat. Hope's body writhed to the blunt, suggestive lyrics she belted out, and the crowd swayed to her every move, screaming out their joy.

I sat down in my assigned seat and drank it in, loving every moment of the performance, thrilled to be a part of the audience for this one time. I let my mind wander where it would, unsure of my next move.

I'd lost at least four or five hours somehow. I thought back to that timeless falling I'd done after entering the portal. Then I thought about how easy my escape had been, limping across the Arch plaza. Something strange had to have happened when I followed Coral into the portal, that was the only explanation.

I thought about Coral, disappearing into the portal, maybe to fascist Achse, maybe to some other 'verse. I hoped they were okay. I suppose anywhere was better than being enslaved to maintain that link to Achse, imprisoned in a coffin-like tank half full of scummy water. Still, my worry for Coral sat heavy in my abdomen, a lump of guilt and urgency to tell Hope. I didn't know what my crew's leader could do about the situation, but I had the feeling she needed to know and would have more wisdom to do something with it than I did.

The stage lights brightened from blue, past green, to a sunny yellow as Dribbler picked up the pace on the drums and Hope moved on to "Since You're Gone" by The Cars. A cluster of college-aged Deltans near me shrieked with glee. Who knew that The Cars were big in Delta these days?

The song choice made me wonder if the crew missed me. I'd rushed out, kind of stupidly when I'd gotten embarrassed. Even thinking about how I'd left brought that uneasiness back to me. Maybe they'd written me off as fragile and sensitive? Would I be able to face them without freaking out again?

And then, a familiar shade of blue caught my eye, down at the center of the balcony. In a boxed-in area full of electronic consoles, keyboards, and blinking lights, sat my twin. Delta Jules had taken my place, running the lights and sound.

A terrible thought froze me from head to toe: what if they hadn't even noticed? What if the other Jules had sent me off on a fool's errand to usurp me? Maybe their plan all along was to infiltrate Hope's Tour? Or had they simply wanted to escape their world the way I had escaped my own?

I seethed, sitting there in the back of the house. My hands balled into fists, my face heated up, and all I could do was stare daggers into the back of my doppelganger's spiky blue head.

As I was just about to leap from my seat to confront the usurper, claws bit into my legs as Jasmine the cat appeared out of the darkness to climb up into my lap. She stuck her nose up to touch my nose, sniffing with her mouth slightly open. She let out a "prrrt!" and head-butted my cheek.

Surprised, I let out a squeak and ruffled the fur on top of her head affectionately. "Jazzy! Hey there sweetie, looks like you found me!"

The genetically enhanced cat met my eyes and nodded, her expression seeming serious to my eyes. She hopped down to the floor and ran to the end of the row, unnoticed by the people sitting there. She paused and looked back at me, eyes reflectively glowing in the darkness as she waited for me.

I rose from my seat to follow, and she disappeared down the aisle, downward towards the stairway to the lower levels of the theater. I rushed after her, feeling a bit of déjà vu as I chased her past rows and rows of seats, along the edge of the Harmony theater. We reached the front, where a steel door stood open; behind it, stairs led upwards to the backstage area. Unfortunately for me, a beefy woman blocked the door. She wore a SECURITY t-shirt, chunky goggle Specs, and what might be a stun gun in a holster at her hip.

Jasmine slipped past the guard with no problem, but I wasn't so quick or small. The guard reached out a hand and said, "Where do you think you're going, Scooter?"

I pulled off my stocking cap and ran my fingers through my blue hair. "I'm, uh, with the band. My name's Jules. Just ask Harlan, the stage manager. Tell him sorry I'm late?"

Jasmine's eyes glowed from behind the guard, halfway up the stairs. She licked her nose in irritation.

The guard touched invisible buttons in midair and spoke to someone else in a hushed tone.

As I stood there, my brain sautéing in nervous anxiety, Hope launched into the Rolling Stones' "Get Off of My Cloud", accompanied by Babs' twangy guitar and Dribbler's rat-a-tat-tat.

They made it almost to the end of that song before the guard grudgingly stood aside. "Harlan wants me to tell you that you have some explaining to do, Scooter."

"My name's Jules."

She shrugged; eyes unreadable behind her blocky Specs. "Sure thing, Scooter."

I glared at her as I pushed past to follow Jasmine up the stairs. At the top, we were met with Harlan.

Harlan held a revolver in his hand, pointed at my heart. He said, "I don't know who you think you're tryin' to fool, but we've already got one blue-haired Tinkerbell for a stagehand, and she's up in the balcony in the control booth."

"But Harlan!" I protested. "It's me, Jules! The one you hired in Beta! The other one is—"

"Shut up and sit in that there chair," he said, waving his pistol back and forth between me and a battered wooden chair my the pullies of the stage ropes. "Go on, sit! And we'll sort this out in a few minutes."

"But—"

"You're not makin' your case by yappin'. I said hush!" He pushed his Specs up and locked eyes with me. He pointed the muzzle of the pistol at my forehead for a terrifying little eternity until I nodded wordlessly.

As I sat, he bound me to the back of the chair with duct tape, around my arms and chest, several times. I thought I could get out of the binding, but not quickly, and not quietly.

While he worked at this, he talked over the Specs to others. "Intermission after this song! Crew meeting backstage. Yes, you too, come on down, we have a problem."

Jasmine sat at my feet and stared up at me with huge eyes. She let out a long, mournful cry. "Mrrrroooowwww!"

Harlan spoke to Jasmine without looking at her. "Don't you give me none of that either, missy. I know who she looks like. You outta know by now, that don't mean she's the right one. Why, there was that time we ran into another one of *me* in Tierra. Damndest thing. Can't trust alts none. Never who you think they are."

Jasmine continued to stare at me, sitting upright and tense.

Marcy appeared from elsewhere backstage. She looked from Harlan to me and back and pressed her lips into a tight line.

Hope and the band trailed off to thunderous applause and whistles from the audience. Hope's voice carried backstage, saying, "Don't go anywhere, we're going to take a short break. We'll be right back."

Moments later, Hope, Babs, and Dribbler swept offstage and stood behind Harlan, who still covered me with the handgun.

"What are you doing, Harlan?" cried Hope, putting a hand on the stage manager's shoulder. "Jules is part of our crew! They're family!"

"Yeah, then who's that?" asked Harlan, jerking his chin to point at Delta Jules, who came up the stairs wearing my magenta dress, and the pair of Specs I'd been issued this morning. "What's going on—oh shit, it's me."

Harlan tossed the roll of duct tape to Babs. "Bind that one too, 'till we get this sorted."

Delta Jules took a half step back towards the stairs, and if it were me, I'd be thinking of making a run for it. But if it were me, I wouldn't have any reason to run, since I'm the real Jules. I think they came to the same decision since they allowed Babs to bind their hands in front of them. "Sorry," she said, looking back and forth between my twin and me.

"Ya know, this is pretty stupid," said Dribbler. "I mean, we'd *know* if we'd been working with an impostor, wouldn't we?"

Babs shook her head. "No. I don't know about that. Remember the other Harlan?"

Marcy objected. "That guy was nothing like our Harlan. Wasn't even military. He was a mechanic. I'd have hired him too, except one Harlan's more than enough."

Hope sang, "Why do you have a gun, Harlan? Surely neither Jules is violent?"

Harlan scowled. "Don't think so? What about that *other* Jules, from Erde? Tried to blow up the whole bus. Close call as it was."

Delta Jules spoke up. "They look just like me, sure. But I'm the real Jules, Hope. Please believe me!"

Hope examined the other Jules, then turned to look at me and sang, "You haven't said anything in your defense so far. What do you want here?"

I looked from Hope to Harlan and back. "I was asked, at gunpoint, to be quiet. My defense is, I ran off like a hothead this morning and got tricked into a Parent Trap situation, and now they're trying to steal my life."

Hope stepped closer to me, her dark eyes as serious as I'd ever seen them. "And why would they want to do that?"

I shrugged. "I don't know. To get closer to you, maybe? To frame me for something they did? Just running away to join the circus-like I did?"

She nodded. "And if this is so, where have you been during all this?"

"They gave me their Specs, with a map, which led me to another Tristellian. One named Coral."

Hope backed two steps away from me, her mouth hanging open in shock. "Coral? Are you certain of that name?"

When I nodded, she whirled to face the other Jules. "One of you knows more about this, and I need to know it."

Delta Jules lost color in their face and stammered out, "I—I don't know anything about this."

I continued. "Coral was imprisoned in a tank, hooked up to machines. They said that they were needed to keep the Arch gate open to Achse. I freed them."

Hope let out squeals and clicks just as Coral had, then sang, "You freed Coral? Then where is he?"

"He ran away when guards came after us. Into the portal. I wasn't able to follow."

"And yet you escaped?"

I nodded. "I emerged on the other side, still here in Delta, but several hours later. I have no explanation for that."

Hope frowned but continued to study me.

Harlan snorted, keeping his pistol aimed in my general direction. "It sounds like a tall tale to me."

Jasmine left her spot at my feet and crept over to the other Jules and sniffed their ankles.

Delta Jules took another half step back, to get away from Jasmine. "Look, I've been here the whole time, other than my brunch with Patrick."

"Was Patrick in on this too?" I asked. "He did seem kind of nervous."

"In on what?" asked Delta Jules, their face a textbook study in innocence.

Jasmine trotted back over to me after inspecting the other Jules. She hopped up into my lap and perched there, facing out to the room.

"I think I know how to solve this," sang Hope. "Each of you must tell me who you have a crush on, and that will reveal which is the real Jules."

"You!" blurted out the other Jules. "I didn't want to say, but I'm about half in love with you, Hope."

Hope smiled and walked closer to my twin. "I thought so." From their side, she looked at me. "And you?"

My heart beat a rapid tattoo, and I broke out into a cold sweat. "Do I really have to say?"

Hope nodded.

"Well, I've got a crush on you, and Dribbler, and even a little one on Babs."

"What!" cried Marcy Davenport. "Not me?"

"I, uh," I stammered, "I mean I like you, Marcy, but we haven't gotten *close* enough for me to feel—"

Marcy laughed and crossed over to me and used a box knife to cut me free of the duct tape. Babs locked Delta Jules in a chokehold. Harlan lowered his pistol, his eyes hooded and dark below his furrowed brow.

"Wait. So, you know I'm me?"

Hope laughed. "Yes, we know. *I* knew as soon as I came backstage."

The other Jules exclaimed, "But how?"

Hope smiled and put a hand down near floor level. Jasmine leaped out of my lap and rubbed up against Hope's mitten-like hand and purred loud enough that I could hear her eight feet away. "I trust Jasmine's instincts. And her sense of smell."

I stood up, and let Marcy put her arm around me. "Then why did you ask that question?"

Dribbler laughed. "She just wanted to know how you felt after you ran off this morning. We all wondered what was goin' on with you, and now we know. Plus, your adorable blush gave you away. The other one tried too hard to seem sure."

"Now," sang Hope to the other Jules. "What we do with you depends on what you tell us about why you're here. And how you can help us get away to another 'verse."

"I was trying to do the right thing," said the other Jules, their eyes pleading with us to believe them.

Before anyone else could ask a question, I got in their face and said, "By setting me up? How's that doing the right thing? Making me take the fall for something that you thought needed doing isn't right. You should have done it yourself."

Delta Jules closed their eyes and nodded. "I know, I know. I figured I'd hitch a ride out of Delta and eventually they'd figure out that you're not me and let you go."

They opened their eyes to look into mine and murmured, "win-win, right?"

Rage flooded through me and I pulled back a hand to strike the coward. They winced in anticipation, but the blow never landed. Instead, I let out a strangled growl and stalked off, fighting back angry tears.

Dribbler intercepted me and put his arms around me. I let him hold me while I shook.

"Pity you chose this route," sang Hope. "If you had only told us about Coral's captivity, we would have helped willingly. But now, we have deception between us. Trickery. And we are all in danger. And we cannot escape through the main Arch gate, it will be watched, especially since they know we have Jules. Perhaps they already know we have both of you."

My twin said, "I know another way. An older, smaller portal. I think I can get us out that way."

Marcy said, "Get *us* out? What makes you think you're going with us?"

"No way," I hissed. "We're not taking that backstabber with us."

Hope held up a hand, looking right at me with her deep eyes. She sang, "Jules, let's hear them out. We need to escape as soon as possible. I don't even want to finish the concert but ending abruptly would sound even more alarms."

I scowled at her. "How could you, Hope? They betrayed me. How do you know they won't do it again?"

Hope approached me and put both hands on my cheeks, even as Dribbler's arms encircled me from behind. She put her face an inch from my own and whispered, "I would not, except the Arch Authority, which uses my kind to stabilize their portals, is now down one Tristellian, and I am the obvious replacement. Do you wish to see me in that tank?"

"N-no," I replied, warring within myself.

She leaned forward just a touch and kissed me. Her lips were wide and firm and warm upon mine. The rage within me transformed into a softer, but just as powerful emotion, and I let myself get lost in that kiss. When she withdrew, she whispered, "Please trust me, Jules. This other you will not get the chance to betray you, or us. Besides, being you, they cannot truly be evil. We just do not understand all that is behind their actions."

As her hands left my face, I nodded. "Okay, Hope."

"I'm with Jules. Our Jules, that is," said Marcy. "I don't trust the other one, and I don't want a trickster like that coming along with us."

Babs folded her arms and nodded. "Me neither. No way. Sorry, Hope, but I don't want them on *La Esperanza*."

Harlan looked like he wanted to say something, but he and Hope exchanged a long look, and instead, he dropped his gaze to the floor, his eyes hooded and dark.

Behind me, Dribbler said, "I'm with the others. They can't be trusted."

Jasmine the cat rubbed up against my legs, then let out a long, sad yowl. "Mroooooh!"

Hope crossed to Delta Jules and put one hand on their shoulder and turned to face the rest of her crew. "What shall we do, then? We have to finish the show, and we have to get out of this 'verse. This other Jules, as untrustworthy as they may be, is our only real hope of escape."

Delta Jules blurted out, "I-I don't have to come along very far with you. Just to the next place. Drop me off in Achse, even, I don't care."

"What if you could stay here," I said. "Why not just blame me, an outside agent, masquerading as you? I only barely fooled your spouses into believing that I was you anyway. Maybe we could leave you tied up at the gate. It would all be true. You never told me to free Coral, I did that on my own."

My doppelganger locked eyes with me. "Yeah? How do I explain where I was all day?"

I shrugged. "Maybe you tell them you wanted to get more information on Hope, to help capture her, but it went all wrong and we figured you out? I mean, don't you want to go back to your life?"

The other Jules smiled. "Funny question. I could ask you the same thing."

I laughed. "I hardly think we're in the same situation. You *have* Sam and Patrick. You've made it *work* with them, somehow, where I didn't. And speaking of Patrick, how did you manage to get my Patrick in on this? Or was that your Patrick pretending to be him?"

They shook their head. "No, that wasn't my doing. I thought he might ruin my chances of getting you alone to make the switch. I think he suspected something was up, honestly, but I convinced him to go back to Beta. I told him that I—I mean, you—would get in touch with him soon. I hinted that Hope's Tour might be coming back around to Beta and that you might try to make things right with your Sam when it did."

I cried, "I can't believe you'd—!" but I was cut off by Marcy.

She looked at Delta Jules. "Look, the crowd's getting restless, and we're out of time. Can you make that work?"

The other Jules hesitated, then nodded. "Okay, but leave me these basic Specs at least? They'll help back up my story, and I won't have to wait hours to be discovered."

Babs shook her head and started to retort, but Marcy stopped her by holding up a hand. "Sure. But our Jules will hang onto Specs until we leave. Then we'll leave them off and out of easy reach. Give us a little head start, and make your story more believable, too. Okay?"

With a nod, they agreed.

"We'll need to swap clothes again," I said to my twin, as Dribbler loosened his comforting hold on me.

"What? Why?"

"Because I'm finishing out the show while Marcy keeps you under guard backstage, and it wouldn't do to have a sudden costume change by the stage crew. Besides, I like that dress, you can't keep it."

By the time we'd finished changing clothes, the crowd began chanting in unison. "We want the show! Bring back Hope! We want the show! Bring back Hope!"

I made my way back up to the balcony booth, wearing the Specs I'd been given when we arrived. With them on, the Harmony theater glowed with seemingly magical gilding everywhere. The virtual augmentation transformed the somewhat plain old venue into a palace of wonders; I had to turn down the opacity on my Specs to twenty percent to keep from being overwhelmed by the grandeur superimposed upon the walls and edging.

Okay, I'm lying. My mind wasn't on the augmented reality of the Harmony theater. Nor was it on the dangers that could be lurking within the crowd or outside the venue. No, my mind whirled at excitement at that kiss from Hope, and the wonderful safe feeling of Dribbler's arms around me. I mean, I had no idea what to *do* with those thoughts and feelings, nor did I have any idea what might happen next. I did feel light as air. My embarrassment from this morning, and then again from having to reveal my crushes backstage, had all dissolved into thin air with that wonderful kiss, that reassuring embrace.

Sure, the other Jules had both Sam and Patrick, but I wouldn't swap lives with them for anything. The future seemed full of exciting possibilities.

And Harlan's cue came over the Specs at the perfect time, as I sat behind the consoles; I lowered the house lights and raised the stage lights, revealing Dribbler at his drum set, and Babs wielding her electric guitar like a rock goddess. I left the main spotlight dark until I got the signal, then made Hope seem to materialize in a dazzling spotlight of intense blue. Babs punctuated Hope's appearance with a stinging electric riff that had the audience on their feet, screaming in joy.

Hope touched the mic in its stand before her and sang, "Thank you, everyone! And since you're all standing, it's now time to do our anthem!"

Dribbler and Babs exchanged a look, a nod, and a grin, then the two of them launched into an intricate rhythm and melody, flirting and teasing one another in what sounded like a kind of tango.

I'll admit, I didn't know the song, so I was as mystified as anyone there as Hope began to sing. Her words came as protestations of being mistreated by us, the audience, admitting her frailties, seeming to cry even as her voice reached for the rafters and tore down the hearts of everyone who could hear her, proclaiming that she was "almost human", despite what we might think. Through the song, Hope pleaded with us to see her as worthy of being treated as one of us.

I wept, there in the control booth, her words tearing at me as though I'd wronged her myself. I wanted to cry out to her to tell her she wasn't merely human, but so much more.

I'm not always great at reading crowds, but the energy of the auditorium surrounding me fairly crackled with the same feeling. People cried out things like, "I love you, Hope!" or "You're so beautiful!"

The tone of the song shifted from accusation and self-flagellation to a more tender and powerful declaration of Hope's humanity, inviting us to touch her, but not to touch her, but also, to touch her.

At the end, Dribbler stopped the rhythm and Babs plucked at her strings one at a time in a playful way, then she did a long, sad electric slide as Hope bowed her head at the mic.

Movement out of the corner of my eye broke the spell of the song. Someone ran down the far-right aisle on the mezzanine floor. Someone carrying something long and straight.

I killed all the stage lights to protect Hope. I called out a warning over the private channel on my Specs. "Trouble incoming! Stage left! Get down!"

I brought the house lights up.

A shot rang out, and the soundboard next to me exploded. Bits of plastic and metal showered me as I fell to the floor. Had I not had the Specs on, some of the shrapnel that bounced off of the virtual reality glasses could have blinded me.

Harlan's voice crackled over the Specs. "Jules, are you okay?"

I decided not to reply, in case my voice might give away my position. Instead, I crawled out of the booth and slunk down the row of seats, moving away from the gunman. People scattered out of my way, and I warned them to keep down as well.

A man got on the PA system, asking people to stay where they were, saying the situation was under control.

I heard another shot go off, amid screaming and fighting that now erupted in the Harmony theater. This time, nothing exploded near me, and I fought my way through a stampede of concertgoers, down the left-hand aisle to the stage right door. The guard who'd called me "Scooter" wasn't there, but the metal door had been shut. I banged on it, keeping my head down. Over the private channel on my Specs, I said, "Harlan, I'm at the door, let me in!"

The door opened. Rather than a greeting from Harlan, Zamboni the robot grabbed me up in his powerful metal arms and carried me up the stairs at a run. I protested, but the robot ignored my cries.

Ahead of us, I watched the rest of the crew already running out an emergency exit door at the back of the backstage area. Hope held the door open as Babs carried her guitar and dragged the other Jules out, followed by Dribbler, who carried one of his drums, stand still attached.

Hope scolded them for bringing instruments, then let out a burst of clicks and whistles as Zamboni placed me in front of her. The robot said, "Here they are. Get in the bus. I'll drive."

And with that, we fled the Harmony theater, boarding the tour bus *La Esperanza* as though the hounds of Hell were nipping at our heels.

The next few minutes were a blur as we hustled into Hope's touring van, *La Esperanza*, and then hung on tight as Zamboni burned rubber getting us out of there. We emerged from the underground parking for the Harmony theater to a chorus of car horns and a couple of shrill screams from pedestrians diving out of our way. To be honest, I didn't get a good look at what happened next, because I had thrown myself into a seat next to Hope and had to hold on to keep from being thrown around the cabin.

Hope held on tight to me as well. I hoped I comforted her as much as she comforted me right then. Her solid body, her strong arms, her smooth cool skin, all helped me through the chaos of our escape.

A few blocks later, we plunged into another tunnel, an underground highway, lined by continuous lighting bars up above. I thought it strange that we had the highway mostly to ourselves since traffic elsewhere never seemed to let up.

I wondered where the other Jules might be, but then I caught a glimpse of them up in the driver's compartment with our robot driver. At one point, we veered onto an offramp that led even further down into the depths below Delta's version of Chicago. The lights here were sparse and yellow, like old sodium lights back home. The tunnel was narrow, not much wider than the lane we drove in. I hoped it ran in only one direction.

Dribbler broke the silence. "Where's that twin of yours takin' us, Jules? This don't look like we're goin' anywhere near the Arch."

Reluctantly, I detached myself from Hope's wonderful embrace and held up my hands, palms upward. "How should I know?"

Dribbler frowned. "I got a bad feelin' about this. What if it's a trap?"

Harlan cleared his throat, standing in the aisle, feet spread apart enough to brace him for the movements of the bus. He gestured in the direction of the other Jules with the long rifle he held close to his body. "I reckon if it's a trap, that someone's gonna have some new holes to worry about."

Babs stood up from her seat and pumped a fist. "Yes! I'm with you, Harlan. We will kick some ass if it comes to that."

"I do not wish harm on the other Jules," sang Hope. "Let us try to find other ways to resolve such a situation. If it is a trap, the other Jules has no way of notifying anyone where we are and where we are going."

Marcy shook her head. "Maybe not, but maybe it was arranged ahead of time? Maybe the yahoo with the gun in the theater was meant to flush us out and then Jules would take us to someplace specific for capture?"

There was a pause while we all considered that. Then, I spoke up. "Could they know that Jules would be revealed? That we'd trust them to take us somewhere like that? I can't picture setting something like this up in advance."

Hope touched my arm and sang, "If you do not imagine it as something you might think of, then perhaps this means it is not something this other Jules would do, either."

I sighed. "Sure, but I wouldn't have done a lot of things this Jules has done."

She smiled and squeezed my arm. "Of course you wouldn't, love. This is why you are the superior Jules in every way. But I get the feeling your twin is being forced into action."

The bus slowed towards a stop. We all looked forward and saw that there was a checkpoint or toll booth ahead.

"Betcha this is the trap," growled Harlan.

Babs leaped across the cabin, flattening herself against the wall next to the side exit door. "Don't know about you, but I'm kinda looking forward to it!"

"Babs, hold on," sang Hope.

I stood up and started toward the front of the bus to have a word with my twin.

"Jules, no!" barked Harlan, waving me away with the barrel of his rifle. "I won't be able to tell you and the other one apart if I need to. Scoot."

I met Harlan's eyes and saw something dark in them. This soldier meant business. I held up my hands and stepped aside. "If you say so, Mister Harper."

"'Sides," he said in a softer tone. "If this is legit, how ya think them at the booth'll react to two of you together?"

I made my way back to Hope, who stood and took my hand. "Harlan is right. If Delta Jules is being honest with us, you need to stay hidden for now. If this is a trap, perhaps you should go upstairs for a bit?"

I shook my head and held her hand firmly in mine. "No. I'm not letting all of you take that risk without me."

Marcy and Hope exchanged a look. Marcy said, "Look, Jules, that's very brave of you and all, but you'll put us in danger. At least go back into the kitchenette in case someone boards and takes a half-assed look around?"

The bus stopped. Hope pulled me back toward the other room, no room for argument in her stride. I let her pull me, and couldn't think of anything useful to say as she opened the door and motioned me in.

And then, Zamboni's voice buzzed over the intercom speakers. "We have been confirmed as guests of Jules Martin. We may proceed into the complex."

Hope and I stared at each other. I said, "The complex?"

She touched her snout with both flipper-hands in that Tristellian shrug of hers and sang, "I do not know, either, Jules."

She started to turn to rejoin the others, but I stopped her with a light touch on her shoulder. She faced me, smiling, and waited.

"H-Hope," I stammered. "Thank you for recognizing the real me. I was afraid—"

She reached to pull me into an embrace, and I welcomed the hug. She sang, "My kind has traveled other worlds long enough that we know how to tell souls apart, despite appearances. I know you, Jules. I see you."

When I turned my head to look her in the eyes, she met me with another kiss. I let myself get lost in her embrace, her kiss, for a long moment. The rest of the 'verse could take care of itself for a bit.

Harlan called from up front. "Hope! The robot and the other one need ya in the driver's compartment!"

She slipped away from me, leaving me warm and a little confused. So, I followed in her wake.

"I can not comply with this command," stated Zamboni, bringing the bus to a halt, seemingly nose to nose with another, identical bus in front of us. I saw the other Jules and myself behind that windshield, as well as Delta Jules in this compartment with Zamboni, Hope, and myself. This did not help my confusion at all.

The mirrored surface of the portal was contained in an Arch barely bigger than *La Esperanza* herself. It would be a tight squeeze driving through there.

Their face red with some upset, my twin let out an exasperated sigh. "Look, we don't have time for this, let's just drive on through!"

"Where does the portal go?" asked Hope.

Delta Jules turned to face Hope and stammered, "I-I'm not sure. It's exploratory, and it's not guided by a mind—"

"—Like a Tristellian? Like Coral?" sang Hope, a dangerous note in her voice.

My twin nodded and swallowed hard before continuing. "Yes. Your people are attuned to the paths between the worlds. Our machines can only do so much. Most expeditions through this portal never return. But it's all we had before—"

Hope raised her voice now, visibly trembling. "—Before enslaving my *people* to make your machines work better? To make the Arch Authority wealthy beyond imagining?"

I touched Hope's upper arm with my fingers, to lend support, but she shook me off.

Delta Jules' eyes widened, and they held up hands between themself and Hope. "I didn't—I couldn't—It wasn't me—I did what I could—"

Hope breathed in deep, and I thought she might scream at the other me, but instead let her breath out in a whistling gust, making her headscarf flutter around her as she deflated. She sang, much quieter, but still with danger in her tone. "Well, we are in luck, I am a Tristellian. If this portal goes to the paths between the worlds, I can guide us. *You* are no longer needed, Jules Martin of Delta Earth."

"P-please, Hope, don't leave me here!"

Hope's eyes narrowed. "If you had approached us openly, we likely would have brought you with us. Your fate, for tricking us, is to remain in your world and try to undo the Arch Authority's enslavement of Tristellians from within the organization. And know this; I see you now. I will always see you as different from *my* Jules, or any other Jules we encounter. Do not try this trick again."

Delta Jules wept and nodded. "I'm sorry, so sorry. I'll do everything I can to free Tristellians. B-but they have captives in every Arch world. I don't know how—"

Hope cut them off. "Do what you can. Recruit others. Make a *difference*, Jules."

"I tried! The whole idea was to warn you—"

"Warn us?" I cried. "You sent me in, unprepared, not knowing I was even in danger!"

The other Jules' eyes flashed anger at me. "You *knew*! You arrived in Delta on the run. I needed you to know that Hope, personally, was in danger, so you could save her. That's how I was going to make a difference!"

"And instead, I did what you should have done, I freed Coral. You could have done what I did, and easier, any day you liked!"

Hope took my hand with one of hers and pointed out of the cabin with her other hand. To Delta Jules, she sang, "I do not doubt your heart or your intentions. But I can not abide deception. We can not trust you. Now, go from my bus. And to begin making a difference, do what you can to give us a head start."

Delta Jules slouched past Hope but snatched the Specs off the top of my head as they passed me. I let them since they'd need them more than I would.

Hope pressed a button on the console, and her voice echoed from all over the bus's intercom system. "Secure yourselves, this will be a bumpy ride. We shall drive through the portal as soon as the hatch has closed from letting our guest depart."

"Hope," I said, "What about tying them up like we talked about?"

She shook her head. "As they said, we have no time. And there's little they can do before we leave, anyway. I don't trust them, but I know that *you* wouldn't betray us to the authorities, and perhaps they don't have it in them to do so either. They would have done so already if they were going to. They had ample opportunity. Now, sit down and hang on."

"They're out!" shouted Dribbler as I heard the side hatch close.

"Mister Zamboni, would you please take us through the portal?"

"By your command," said the robot, and the bus crawled forward, toward our reflection.

Red lights flashed all around us, accompanied by a klaxon.

"Shit!" cried, Dribbler. "They sold us out already!"

I peered out both side windows but saw no sign of my doppelganger; instead, I watched as a half dozen soldiers in Arch Authority uniforms dashed into the chamber and drew pistols from their belts. They were followed by an armored car with the double-A logo on its hood and a gun turret on its roof. I grabbed Hope's hand and pulled her down to the floor with me. "Everybody down! We've got company!"

Harlan slung his rifle into a holster that ran diagonally across his back, then dashed for the stairway. "I'll give 'em somethin' to think about from upstairs!"

Gunshots, along with the *pang* of bullets pelting *La Esperanza's* hull, filled the air with a deafening cacophony. Marcy screamed as an impact cracked one of the side windows into a spiderweb. Babs swore rapid-fire in Spanish. Harlan's rifle reported from somewhere up top.

The bus began to crawl forward, and as I watched, the mirrored curtain swallowed up Zamboni, Hope, and then washed over me. As it did, the noise and terror of the firefight vanished, leaving me in jarring silence. I couldn't see or hear anything at first, then only an impression of colored lights and movement. I felt I couldn't trust my senses; I could hear my voice and the voices of others, chanting and singing something in an alien tongue.

Hope's hand in mine provided the only constant, and we clung to each other, weathering the storm of traversal together.

And then, we were through, in the nowhere land between worlds. Zamboni, impassive as ever, drove the bus. Hope stood and helped me up as well. I kept ahold of her hand, since the world seemed unsteady and a bit unreal to me right then.

"Where," I said with a gasp, "I mean, what is going to happen to us? What was the Gate set for?"

"Unknown," said Zamboni.

"How long will we be in between?"

"Unknown," repeated Zamboni.

"What? Are we lost?"

Hope squeezed my hand and sat in the co-pilot's seat. She sang, "You forget, I can guide us through the ways between the worlds. It is why my people are so valuable to the Arch Authority, it seems."

"You can?" I thought back to Coral disappearing into the inactive portal, leaving me behind in Delta. "Well, lucky we have you along, then."

She smiled and let go of my hand and turned to stare out the front. She sang, "Your trust in me is wonderful, Jules. I did not say I knew where I was going, or how to get there. But we will end up somewhere. I shall guide us. It will take concentration, however."

I nodded. "Okay. I'll go check on the others."

As I entered the main cabin, I discovered Marcy, Dribbler, and Babs sitting on one side couch, their expressions dazed and glassy.

Before I could say anything to them, Harlan's voice came over the intercom. "I could use a li'l help up here! Jules, bring some of the pyrotechnics from the back. And shake a leg!"

To my surprise, after the intercom cut off, I heard Harlan's rifle fire several times, answered by a deeper-throated gun somewhere behind us.

I dashed past the kitchen area to the aft hatch into our supplies and grabbed a fireproof case containing some of our stage pyrotechnics. Despite its bulk, I made it up the stairs in record time. The ladder to the roof extended into the hallway of the upstairs, and my ears rang with the next volley of gunfire. Harlan fell from his perch and landed heavily next to me. I could hear the wind whoosh out of his chest, and his eyes bugged out with the sudden landing.

"Harlan! Are you—"

Harlan waved a hand. "Ahm fine," he wheezed. "Jes fine. I'll mind myself. Now, get on up there -gasp- and toss out some smoke bombs. Number twos should do it."

I tore open the case, grabbed up an armful of the dark cylinders, and climbed to the top of the ladder. "So, they followed us? How?"

Harlan, on his hands and knees now, coughed and spat, then yelled at me, "Never mind that, jes get up there!"

I peeked my head out of the hatch, and sure enough, the armored car followed us through the maelstrom, maybe a hundred feet behind us. As I pulled the igniter on three of the smoke bombs, I spied movement out of the corner of my eye. "Harlan! There's someone—"

Something slammed into the back of my head, and everything went black for a moment. The next thing I knew, arms hooked under my shoulders, and someone hauled me up on top of the bus. The air filled with blue, red, and yellow smoke.

While I struggled against wooziness, I did my best to grab onto my assailant, but only managed to twist around to face them.

It was me. The other me, Delta Jules, almost unrecognizable with an angry snarl twisting their face. They shoved at me, and my feet began to slide out from under me. They growled and said, "Now you can see what it's like to be tossed out like yesterday's garbage!"

The other Jules shoved, and my feet lost purchase on *La Esperanza's* slick hull. As I fell, I managed to grab onto one of their ankles. I thought maybe I might be able to stop from falling off into chaos, but my twin's footing slipped out from under them, and I had the satisfaction of hearing them fall to a heap on the roof.

And then, I hit the ground and had to roll to keep from being run over by Hope's tour bus. The smoke from the bombs swirled around me, and the armored car's engine roared up from close behind.

Just then, a slice of sunlight cut through the colorful smoke, and a vertical rip in space showed me another world, as if behind a curtain.

The armored car's guns blasted another couple of potshots at the tour bus, and one wayward shell passed far too close to me for my comfort. Sand rained down on me, and the smoke began to clear.

I only had one chance. I dove for the rip, and into another world.

Chapter 17 – Stop Breakin' Down Blues

As I fell through the rip in space-time, I braced for a rough landing, hoping to roll as I hit the ground on the other side.

Except I kept falling.

The world spun on an axis somewhere above my head. Water and grey sky traded positions faster than my eyes could follow. A flash of a familiar skyline between eye-blinks gave faint reassurance, but I had no time to consider that when the water rose to slam into me, hard and cold.

The impact forced air from my lungs, and the ashen light from the sky faded from view as the surface receded out of my clawing reach. As I sank, I lost any sense of which way might be up or down.

Then, I blacked out, certain that I'd escaped an explosive death at the hands of the Arch troopers, only to trade it for drowning alone in another world.

I don't recall any dreams, but I did awaken with the impression of having dreamed a long while. The first thing I noticed upon waking up was that the hard bed I lay upon moved up and down, like *La Esperanza* going over hills on the highway. The rumbling of a motor somewhere in the general direction of my feet seemed to confirm that impression. At the same time, a cold wind blew across my face and chilled my damp hair. I trembled with the cold under a scratchy wool blanket, which I realized was my only covering other than my underwear.

I cracked open an eye to see where I was. The horizon, over a railing, bobbed up and down in time with the feeling of motion I'd observed, and a fine spray covered my face in a new layer of chill water. I lay on a padded bench of some kind, and someone sat across a narrow walkway from me on an identical bench, watching me with dark eyes.

The person watching me was a man with facial hair and waist-length hair tied back behind his head. His eyes, filled with concern, narrowed as I opened mine more fully. "Hey, man, are ya gonna live after all?"

The man wore a colorful paisley tunic and black skinny jeans under a bright yellow rain slicker. His face held a deep tan, and other than the beard, he looked exactly like someone I hoped to see.

"D-dribbler?" I croaked. "That you?"

His brow furrowed and he shook his head. "Naw. I don't know any Dribbler. But man, I bet your eggs are scrambled after nearly drownin'. I'm Jimmy, and this is my boat, the *Nickel Ringo*."

"You saved me? Thank you so much. I just have one question."

Jimmy scratched his beard and shrugged. "Go ahead, shoot!"

I took a couple of breaths and pulled the scratchy blanket a bit closer around me. "Where are my clothes?"

Jimmy snorted. "Couldn't leave you in them after fishing you out of Lake Michigan. I didn't think you'd make it even so. Sopping wet clothes out on the lake in November? That's a recipe for hypothermia. After you coughed up a couple of gallons of lake water, I gave you mouth to mouth, stripped you down, and wrapped you up in my boat's emergency blanket."

"Uh, well, thanks again for saving my life, Jimmy." Despite this debt I owed him, I was mortified to know this man had seen me naked.

"Hey, I got a couple of questions for you, too," said Jimmy, taking his eyes from me to peer out over the lake towards the Chicago skyline.

"Uh, shoot," I said.

"Well, guess I should ask your name first."

"I'm Jules. And before you ask, I'm not a boy or a girl, but kind of both. You can use whatever pronouns you're comfortable with for me though."

Jimmy held up both hands, palms toward me, and shook his head. "Hey, man, that's cool, I got no problem with that. You do you, Jules, it's groovy with me. Pleased to meet you. Next question: how the hell did you fall out of the sky like that. I didn't see a plane or a helicopter or even a parachute."

I sighed. "I don't think you'd believe me if I told you."

"Try me. I've seen a lot of crazy shit in my life."

I smiled. "I'm sure you have. Okay, I jumped through a hole between worlds."

Jimmy laughed. "Why'd you do a crazy thing like that?"

"I was being shot at," I said. "It seemed like the best thing to do at the time."

His dark eyes twinkled against the silvery overcast sky. "You do this a lot, jumping from one world to another?"

I grinned. "More than I would have thought, up until a few days ago. Usually, there's an Arch involved."

"Not this time, though?"

I shook my head.

"Okay, I'll bite, what do you mean by an Arch?"

I considered before answering. If he had to ask, this world didn't have an Arch Network. If that were the case, I might very well be marooned here for the rest of my life, unless this reality developed interdimensional travel on their own. Perhaps they already had? Since Jimmy seemed to be an analog of my friend Dribbler, whose first name I knew to be James, I decided to trust him more than another stranger. Even one who'd saved my life.

I sat up, holding the blanket to me, still shivering. "Jimmy, where I come from, there are inter-dimensional portals between parallel universes. There's a corporation that's been building these Arches that you can drive through to go from one version of reality to another. I've met another version of you, he goes by Dribbler because he's a drummer in a band. He's one of my best friends."

Jimmy's eyes opened wider and his mouth hung open for a long moment, then he said, "Another me? How's that possible?"

I shrugged. "There are probably an infinite number of you's out there. I've already met another me and know of at least two other me's as well. I don't know how it's possible, any more than I understand quantum physics. So, I'm guessing you don't have anything like that on this Earth?"

He shook his head. "Naw. That's science fiction here. If anyone here can do it, it's being kept a big secret. So, how do we get you home?"

I shook my head and scanned the sky. I didn't see any rips in reality hovering up there. "Even if the hole I fell through is still there, I don't know how we'd get me up to it. And if you don't have any way to tunnel through to other worlds, I guess I'm stuck here."

Jimmy nodded and watched my face a long while before saying. "I got somethin' to show you, Jules, somethin' I haven't shown to anyone else yet because it's too crazy. But first, let's get you some clothes."

"Yes, please!"

He stood up and opened the bench, which turned out to double as storage, and rummaged around and came up with a yellow sundress, patterned with tiny boats, anchors, and life preservers. He handed this to me and turned to face outward to look at the skyline once more. "Sorry it's out of season, but it's what I've got. You'll want to keep the blanket. Got some flip-flops, too."

"It's pretty," I said, struggling into it while trying to keep the blanket up between Jimmy and myself. "Is it your girlfriend's?"

"Naw, it's mine."

I thought about the tunic he wore under the rain slicker. "So, in this world, clothing isn't gendered?"

He shrugged. "My old man wouldn't be caught dead in a dress, but my generation's a bit more open-minded. I get called Mary-ann by some of the guys at my favorite bar, but I find that dresses can be a great conversation starter. I get more dates than you'd think."

"Girls and boys?" I asked, wincing at the way it sounded after I said it.

He turned around and smiled and nodded. "Sure. And in-between, too, like you. Just how close are you and Dribbler?"

I hated that I could feel color flood my cheeks. "I think you've already guessed. We had a flirtationship going on. I'd hoped to see where else it might lead."

"His loss, my gain?" said Jimmy, winking at me.

I didn't know how to respond to that, so I just said, "Maybe. I'd rather not give up on seeing him again just yet, though I don't see much hope."

He nodded. "Just teasin', Jules. You seem sweet. Now, I'm gonna show you somethin' else I fished out of these waters, and I don't want you to freak out, okay?"

"Sure," I said, "I'm curious to see what you think is going to surprise someone who just fell out of the sky."

"Well, you aren't the first to fall out of the sky. I'd hoped you could shed some light on this since I've been trawlin' around out here lookin' for answers for weeks now. Hang on just a moment." He disappeared into the small cabin on the boat and returned with a bundle shaped like a baby swaddled in a blanket.

The bundle wriggled in his arms like a baby, but the sound it made wasn't human. It was a trilling, squeaking, clicking sort of sound.

A gray muzzle, full of tiny sharp teeth, as well as a pair of wide eyes, poked out of the bundle. The little creature peered at me and let out what sounded to me like a happy squeal.

"A baby Tristellian!" I cried, my heart beating faster within my chest.

Jimmy handed the bundle to me and said, "So you *do* recognize the little critter?"

"This isn't a critter, it's a *person*," I said, smiling at the alien infant. "I know a grown-up person that looks like this darling little baby. She's a Tristellian, from a far-away reality. She's also a rock star, and I'm more than half in love with her. Everybody who meets her is. Her name is Hope."

Jimmy stared at me. "You're just full of surprises, aren't you? I've been callin' this one, Lucy. 'Cause she's a little angel who fell from the sky, just like you. I've been lookin' for others like her, out on the water. Guess I didn't do that, but it can't be a coincidence that you're here now. Maybe we can figure a way to get you both back home, wherever that may be."

I shivered in the cold November air, despite the wool blanket Jimmy'd given me. A chill wind blew across Lake Michigan and the deck of the small boat we stood on. I held the baby Tristellian close to my chest for mutual warmth. I peered up into the leaden sky as if to find a way out of this world.

Jimmy wrung his hands. "Do ya think a solution's just gonna fall out of the sky?"

I laughed. "Why not? I did. Lucy did."

"True! But not all at once."

"You were here both times, though?"

Jimmy nodded. "Yeah, but the first time was a fluke."

"And the second time?"

Jimmy ran a hand through his hair and glanced at the sky before meeting my eyes. "I guess you could call it a gut feeling. Something strange about that patch of lake. I went out when I could, lucky for you."

I smiled. "Very lucky. Almost unbelievably lucky. I mean, what are the odds?"

Jimmy shrugged. "Dunno. Maybe you'd best get a lottery ticket while you can?"

"Maybe! So, if lightning's struck twice, dare I hope for a third time?"

"Aw, would it be so bad to be marooned here with me?" Jimmy winked at me.

I shivered. "Might seem better to me if I could get warm. But that means abandoning the spot where I fell through."

"Thinking of flappin' your arms and flyin' back up there?"

I sighed and slumped. "Guess not."

Jimmy reached out toward me but stopped just short of touching my shoulder. He withdrew his hand. "We'll figure something out. We can come back here, same time tomorrow, okay?"

"Is the time of day important?"

Jimmy nodded. "Yeah, both you and little Lucy there fell into my life at 4:04 pm on a Wednesday."

"Huh. It wasn't a Wednesday or that time of day when I left Delta. There must be a time shift here. Well, and a spatial shift too, since

I was deep below the city somewhere. Er, that's not right, I was between worlds."

Jimmy pressed his lips together and made a popping sound. "Sure. I don't know anything about all that. But let's get you home and in somethin' warmer, maybe have some dinner? Then we'll come back here tomorrow."

Brunch this morning with Patrick seemed years ago. "Good idea. I'm starved!"

Lucy gurgled and wriggled in my arms, letting out a whistling, descending note.

"Sounds like she's hungry too. Let's go!" Jimmy showed me into the boat's cabin, which wasn't any warmer, but I found the lack of wind to be a vast improvement.

My host guided his boat quickly and quietly through the lake. We bobbed on choppy waves kicked up by late afternoon winds, and the city loomed up ahead.

After we pulled up to the dock, Jimmy secured his boat and helped me out onto the dock. From there, we walked to a trolley station. Jimmy bought some hotdogs and glass bottles of soda from a vendor, and I had to exert all my willpower to not wolf it down in seconds. Jimmy fed thumb-sized bits of hotdog to a delighted Lucy, taking care to keep her covered within her blanket.

As we waited for transportation to arrive, I felt conspicuous standing there wrapped in the wool blanket and Jimmy's flimsy sundress. The other people paid no attention, however. I approved of the androgyny of a couple of the others waiting there with us and wondered if this could be the first new world where I might fit in.

Maybe.

"Ey. What's up with the blue hair, guy?" said an older man in a weather-stained trenchcoat and knit beanie featuring an ursine character of some kind.

"Why don't you mind your own business?" said Jimmy, interposing himself between me and the man.

"I can take care of myself," I said to Jimmy. To the trenchcoat-wearing man, I said, "I'm a natural cobalt, what's it to you?"

The guy ignored me and glared at Jimmy. "Flippin' pansies. You ruined my country. Can't even have a car in Chicago anymore because of people like you. Hope you're happy."

Jimmy snorted. "No one's stoppin' you, bud."

"Taxes is what's stoppin' me. Transit laws is what's stoppin' me. Pansies like you are why we gotta wait for trolleys like it was a hundred years ago." The man stepped toward Jimmy.

My new friend stood in place, glaring at the guy.

"Look, if I had a nice hat like yours, you wouldn't even know what color my hair is. But I fell in the lake. Give me a break, okay?"

The man kept his eyes locked with Jimmy, still ignoring me. "Things get a little rough out there on the water?"

"What if they did?" said Jimmy, his eyes narrowing. His hands closed into fists, and the older guy pulled his hands out of his coat pockets and did the same.

To my relief, a trolley pulled up just then. I put my hand on Jimmy's arm, and after another tense moment, trenchcoat boarded the trolley ahead of us.

"Maybe we should wait for the next one," I suggested.

Jimmy shook his head, taking my hand in his, and lead me onto the trolley. "Can't let guys like that get to you. Can't let them win."

I sighed. "He didn't get to *me*, he got to *you*. I appreciate you taking care of me, but I don't need a knight in shining armor. Just a hot shower and a change of clothes and a good night's sleep, maybe?"

We sat, facing each other, still holding hands. Tension flowed out of his face like water draining from a tub. "Yeah. Okay. Sorry."

I shook my head. "No, don't be. I just got shot at and I've been on the run for days now, I didn't want any more trouble. At least, not until I'm more myself."

Jimmy nodded, then his eyes lit up. "D'you suppose there's a Jules like you here in my world?"

I nodded. "Odds seem good since versions of me seem to be all over the multiverse, and I know another you already."

"You think maybe that Jules knows something that could help you? I could check for them in the phone book."

I shrugged. "If you don't have any portals here, I don't see why they *would* know any more than you."

He nodded. "Yeah, I guess not. Still, I'm gonna look them up if we can get you on your way."

I rolled my eyes. "What are you even going to tell them?"

I'd never seen such a wolfish grin cross *my* Dribbler's lips like the one Jimmy gave me. "I'm going to ask them if they believe in fate. And then I'll tell them the truth. From what I know about you, the local Jules is gonna be open-minded, too."

"Never can tell. So far, one of the Jules I met was sketchy enough to work for corporate goons enslaving Lucy's people for their own gain. And another, from a place called Erde, tried to kill my friends. She was a piece of work. Had interesting neo-Victorian fashion sense, though."

"She, hmm?" said Jimmy, raising an eyebrow.

I shrugged. "Yeah, don't ask me. I don't imagine all of my inter-dimensional twins express their gender the same as me. Who knows if they're even configured the same biologically."

"Wouldn't-- wouldn't that mean they're *not* another you, then? If they're *that* different, then how are they even you at all?"

I smiled. "You think I have all the answers? Buddy, I'm swimming as fast as I can, and I still can't keep up with all the weirdness life's been throwing at me since I followed that cat."

"Cat?"

I shook my head. "Long story. Suffice it to say, she was my White Rabbit."

"So, you have Lewis Carroll where you're from, too?"

I nodded. "Seems like different worlds split off at certain points in history. Your world doesn't seem all that different than mine. Seems calmer here though, maybe it's the lack of cell phones?"

"Some people have those. I can't be bothered, I don't want to be reachable all the time."

I smiled. "You'd hate Delta, then. They're not only always available, they're always plugged in. It had some advantages, but it wasn't a calm place."

"This is our stop," said Jimmy, standing up as the trolley pulled up to a station. He pointed down a cross street. "I just live a couple of blocks that way."

We disembarked, and thankfully, trenchcoat-guy stayed on the trolley. Lucy squeaked as the cold wind hit her face once again, and I said, "I hear you, little thing. Not much longer now."

Jimmy led us to his building, and we took the elevator up a couple of floors. His apartment was near the end of the hallway on that floor, and when he let us in, my nose was assaulted by a fishy stink.

"Sorry about the mess," apologized my host, clearing off papers on his love seat just inside the door. "The little squeaker goes through sardines and diapers, and trash pickup's not until tomorrow."

I nodded. "I've got other friends who are single parents. Now, about that shower? And clothes? Please?"

The shower turned out to be a glass stall with an economy showerhead that blasted me with needles of steamy water. I lathered up good and let out a happy sigh as the lake water, sweat, and dirt sloughed off of me.

"I hope you like maroon!" cried Jimmy from the next room. "I left some leggings and a sweater on the counter for you!"

I guessed he must have snuck in and out while I'd been rinsing off, eyes closed. Irritation crept into my otherwise blissful shower, knowing he'd probably had a peek at me. Not that he could see much but an outline through the pebbled glass of the shower stall, but still, I'd rather he'd gotten my consent first.

"That's fine," I called. "Please shut the door? I'd like some privacy, please!"

"No problem!" the door shut and I was alone in the steamy bathroom.

After toweling off, I found the maroon leggings needed to be rolled up at the ankles, but fit comfortably enough. The sweater was a heavy cable-knit baggy thing of nearly the same color, but that suited me just fine. I also liked that it covered me almost to my knees. Cozy.

Hope's voice sang the lyrics to "Almost Human" in my head, and I realized I did feel a hundred percent better. Her voice soothed some of my fears, but at the same time, a lump of something sat heavily in my stomach.

I missed Hope. I missed my Dribbler, and Jasmine, and all my new family on the tour bus.

I realized the lump in my tummy was *homesickness*. Imagine that, homesick for a group of people I'd only known a few days, in a home that moved from place to place.

As nice as Jimmy seemed, as comfortable as this Earth promised to be, I wanted my new family, my new home, back.

But how? Would Hope find a way to drop a rope from the sky for me to climb up? Would I have to parasail up to a hole in the sky over Lake Michigan? Would that even work?

I emerged in a plume of steam from the bathroom, only to be greeted by a giggling naked baby Lucy, crawling across the shag rug towards me.

Jimmy cried, "Get back here, you little twerp! I haven't got your diaper on you yet!"

I scooped up the baby Tristellian and delivered her back to our host. "How do you even do that. You know, with the tail and all?"

"Gotta cut a slit in the back. I use medical tape to hold it together. By the way, man, those clothes look way better on you than they ever did on me. Keep 'em!"

"Thank you, you're an excellent host. I'm just about to pass out. Do you have a blanket and a corner I could curl up in?"

Jimmy's eyes twinkled and he said, "I'd say you could join me, but I guess we don't know each other well enough. Yet. So, you take my bed, and I'll sleep out here on the couch. Gotta feed the little booger in the wee hours anyway, she can't go more than a few hours without eating, it seems."

He showed me his nest of a bed, which I flopped into without comment. He lingered in the doorway a long moment but stayed true to his word and shut the door with me inside.

I don't know how long I slept, but it was dark when I awoke. A strange light glowed at the foot of Jimmy's bed. A large, oval light that shimmered like a sideways pond. For a disoriented moment, I thought Jimmy might have an oval full-length mirror in his room, but this gave off its own light.

A figure, smaller than Jimmy, stood in silhouette inside the glowing oval. The figure wore a full-skirted dress of some kind. The figure also held a bell-muzzled gun that rang alarm bells in my head.

I decided to play possum as she crept closer, to the side of the bed.

When she stood over me, I struck her in the gut as hard as I could. She folded in half, her breath escaping in a whoosh. I leaped to my feet. The gun clattered across the floor, and I dove after it. So did she.

We wrestled on the ground, and she struggled for breath since it seemed I'd knocked the wind out of her. She scratched at my face with sharp, hard nails, as I kicked her in the shins and elbowed her in the ribs.

The portal at the foot of the bed winked out, leaving us in darkness.

From the other room, Lucy wailed as only a baby can. Some thumping around let me know that Jimmy was awake, so I cried out for help.

The gun skittered across the bedroom floor as we wrestled in the dark. I couldn't be certain which way it went, and I hoped my double from Erde didn't know either.

The door opened, and the lights snapped on, and my eyes were too dazzled for a moment for that to be more useful than darkness.

"Jimmy! Grab the gun! Don't shoot it!" I cried, even as my doppelganger let out a scream of frustration, reaching past me for it.

Jimmy kicked the gun out into the hallway and grabbed the Jules from Erde and pulled her off of me. She swung wildly in his grasp. "Let me go! You don't understand!"

"I understand that you're hurting my new friend, bitch!" he yelled. "And I understand that you're in my apartment, and I didn't invite you here!"

"I need that child! And I need to capture that Jules!"

"What do you know about a child?" I asked, clambering to my feet.

Jimmy held her arms pinned to her sides, hugging her tight from behind. "Man, I know you're not gonna take that child away. Jules, get past me, and make sure Lucy's okay."

She kicked at me as I squeezed past to get out of the room. In the hallway, I found Lucy, gurgling and whistling, as she crawled towards the portal gun. I scooped her up, and then grabbed the gun and pointed it into the living room.

"I'm sorry for the mess, Jimmy. It's been good to meet you, but I have to be going now."

Struggling in Jimmy's arms, the Jules from Erde screamed, "No! You can't leave me here!"

Jimmy whipped his head around as I pulled the trigger on the portal gun. "What? Wait!"

Another oval grew in front of me, shimmering with the sunlight of a new day in another world. Before anyone could object, I stepped through, and the portal closed behind me.

Chapter 19 – Walkin' Blues

Have you ever had the feeling of being pulled in two different directions? I don't mean in the figurative sense, of having a difficult decision to make. What I mean is the feeling of physically being tugged in two directions, as though gravity acted from two opposing points.

I can say I had before, though only in dreams. Until now. As I passed through the portal with Lucy, the baby Tristellian, in my arms, it was as though we stood in a hallway that spun around a focal point at my feet, and forces pulled me in both directions at once. I'm trying to convey this in the way that someone just waking from a dream may struggle to describe things that aren't possible in the waking world. This space, this place where we stood, wasn't an actual hallway. It didn't have walls as such. No, it more resembled a tube of some kind, made of the foggy grey nothingness of the space between worlds.

Also, it moved like a living thing. Maybe I'd be better off describing it as the eye of a twister, chaos whirling around a calm center, threatening to tear apart anything that strayed from the path.

At either end of the twister-tunnel stood a portal into a world. I could tell nothing about either one of them, except for what my gut told me in that split second at the center of the storm.

On each side, I had a feeling of home. On the one side, I could imagine a haven, a shelter from the storm. On the other, well, my gut said that while I might be safe, the child might not be. I might be bringing danger along with me.

I admit, in that moment of doubt, I let myself fall towards safety, rather than uncertainty and risk. I might have chosen differently if not for the wriggling, squealing bundle of dolphin-descended baby in my care. My instincts might not be careful when looking out only for myself, but the very most important thing I could do at that moment was to protect Lucy. With my life, if need be.

So, I took a step, and the other portal shrank off into the distance as we fell towards the safer option.

I fully expected another plunge from a height, like the one that led me to Jimmy and Lucy, splashing down in the Lake Michigan of another world.

The multiverse surprised me, yet again.

Falling became dizziness, which cleared bit by bit until I found my feet planted upon a concrete staircase. I took a couple of steps down the stairs, and we emerged into daylight in a familiar place.

The sun shone down on the two of us as a chill wind swept past us. People sat on the stairs, bundled in winter coats, eating sandwiches, poking at smartphones, and talking with one another. Sculptures surrounded the stairs, and I knew that if I looked behind me, I'd see an obelisk-like monument rise to touch the sky.

Indianapolis. Monument Circle. I was home.

Somehow, I knew that *this* Indianapolis was the one I called home; the one in Beta Earth. The one I'd left last week, following a cat, to run away with an alien diva's band. The Indianapolis in the world where I'd left Sam at the altar.

"No," I breathed aloud. "It can't be. I have to find Hope!"

I clipped the portal gun inside my baggy sweater and continued down the stairs until I stood on the bricks that surrounded the Monument. In a daze, shivering without a coat, I found myself walking on automatic. I might be home, but another couple of blocks would take me to a different kind of home, one where I might get some help.

I held Lucy close to my chest and hurried down the sidewalk, away from the Circle, each sign, street name, and business I passed confirming that I'd wound up back on my homeworld of Beta Earth. The thought that it *could* be a very close analog, and not my Beta crossed my mind, but I dismissed it immediately. If I'd been sent home, it wasn't a fake-out version with trivial differences; I could even *smell* that this place was my home.

Well, it used to be, anyway.

I rounded a corner and relief washed over me as the white neon Spyglass sign appeared, marking my most recent place of employment. Probably still could be, if I asked for my job back.

But no, I had other things to do now. And to do them, I needed help from friends.

I pulled open the heavy door to the bar and slipped inside, grateful for the warm humidity that greeted me, along with the *crack* of pool balls hitting each other, and the sour scent of old spilled beer.

"Jules!" cried Maxie, one of the other Spyglass bartenders, peering at me through red cat-eye glasses. "You're fired!"

"I missed you, too, Maxie!" I made my way over to the bar. "Sorry about the lack of notice, but—"

"Save it. I heard you skipped out. Might wanna turn right back around if you know what's good for you," she said, jerking her eyes to one side.

I looked. I groaned. Sam sat at the other end of the bar, her lips pressed into a thin white line, eyes locked onto mine like twin death beams.

"Too late," I said.

Lucy let out a high-pitched squeal of dismay. I patted her and made soft cooing noises. I considered making a break for it before Sam could walk over to confront me, but I knew that without money, cell phone, or even a winter coat, I couldn't walk away.

"Maxie, do you think you could spot me a glass of milk? The little one here is hungry."

Maxie winked at me. "Sure. I'll take it out of your last paycheck."

I waited for Sam to come after me, but she didn't. Instead, she lifted her perfectly manicured hand and pointed at the barstool next to her, her eyes never leaving mine.

I sighed and walked over to my fiancée. Ex-fiancée, I supposed, from the look in her eyes.

"Hi, Sam, how's it going?" I asked, accepting a glass of milk from Maxie. I held it up for Lucy to see, and she grabbed at it with little mitten-hands and tipped it into her muzzle. I'll give her this, she got most of that swallow down her throat. The rest spilled into her blanket. I let her hold the glass as I propped her up on the bar between Sam and myself, as though the baby Tristellian offered shelter from Sam's wrath.

"*How's it going*? How do you *think* it's going? Do you have *any* idea how embarrassed I was when you ran off on our wedding day, Jules? Do you have *any* idea how pissed off Daddy was? Still is."

I nodded. "I know. I'm sorry, Sam. I really am. But I just couldn't—"

She cut me off. "Save it. You could have come to me, Jules. You could have said, 'gee, Sam, I'm just not ready for commitment. I'm not emotionally stable enough to settle down with you like we planned. I need to run away and join the bleeping circus to get it all sorted out first!"

My face flushed hot. "It's not an excuse, but I did try to talk to you. You're always just so *sure* that it'll be fine, we just needed to push ahead, and then we'd just magically live happily ever after."

"I can't *believe*," she hissed, "that you have the utter gall to blame *me* for you leaving me at the altar. Honestly, Jules—"

"No, that's *not* what I'm doing," I spat. "I'm trying to make you understand where I was that day. I didn't *plan* to run off. I wanted to make a go of it with you. But your father—"

"What?" she cried, causing others at the bar to turn to stare at us. "Now you're blaming *Daddy*?"

I closed my eyes and counted to ten, then said, one word at a time. "You know what, Sam? Yes. I *am* blaming him. He never liked me. He told me so, to my face, when you weren't around. Not only that, but I know that he calls me 'it' when he thinks I can't hear him. I heard you talking to him before I left."

Sam, who'd been building up a head of steam to blast me, pulled back and stared at me. "You were eavesdropping?"

I shook my head. "You both had your voices raised, right outside my dressing room. I panicked, Sam. I knew right then that I couldn't join a family that won't give me even the most basic respect. I couldn't stand up there next to you and say with a straight face that I believed we'd be together forever. Not without the support of your family, and not without *you* being willing to stand up for me. I love you, Samantha, and I always will. But I can't put myself in that position. I won't."

"So, you ran," she said, looking at Lucy for the first time. "I see you came back with a souvenir. I don't suppose you managed to have a baby with that alien so soon?"

I had to cough to cover a laugh. Laughing, even at a little joke like that, would be like throwing off sparks in a fireworks factory right now, and I didn't want to get caught in the explosion. "No, this little one doesn't even know Hope, I found her on my own. I figured we were both a bit lost, and both being hunted, so we'd better stick together. As for Hope, I'm thinking she's going to know better than me what to do with a baby of her species."

Sam sighed and looked away, towards the door. "If that's the case, what are you doing back here? Did you forget something?"

"I'm not sure, Sam. I sort of just appeared here. It's a long story."

Still looking at the door, she sighed and said, "You know what, Jules? I don't want to hear your story. And I don't want you back."

Her words stabbed me like an icicle through my heart, but I kept my outward cool. "I didn't come to Beta Earth, or to The Spyglass, to get you back, Sam. I need help to get back to Hope's Tour."

She barked a laugh at me, still looking away. "Of course! I'll call you an Uber! Where is Hope's Tour right now?"

As Lucy finished the small glass of milk, I wiped at her face with a cocktail napkin. "I don't know where they are. Not likely here on Beta."

"What do you want from me? An interdimensional bus pass? If it'll get you gone again, I'm sure Daddy'll pay me back for footing the bill."

I allowed myself a chuckle. "I might just take you up on that if I can figure out where else they might be."

"I don't know what else you want from me," said Sam.

"Why are you staring at the door like that?"

"I'm expecting someone," she said, standing up as the door opened. "I'd introduce you, but I think you two know each other, at least in some bizarre way."

Someone entered The Spyglass. A short man, wearing a leather jacket and stylish boots, strode in, smiling at Sam, then frowning at me. He ran a hand through his shock of blue hair and shook his head in disbelief.

Before me stood yet another doppelganger.

Sam looked from one to the other of us and said, "Jules, meet Jules."

I stared at my double, and said, "Gamma Jules, I presume? I have *got* to watch what I say in the future. It looks like you might just be having better luck with my life than I did, after all!"

"I don't care what you do to me, but you are *not* taking this baby away from me!" I ignored the pained looks that Sam and my double gave me and kept my voice at a level that everyone at the bar could hear. I figured it was my only protection.

"Look, ah, Jules," said Gamma Jules, forcing a smile. "It's not that *we* want the baby. It's that we know that the *Arch* people would do just about anything to get their hands on it."

"She," I said. "Lucy's a *she*, not an *it*." Sam refused to meet my eyes with hers as I said this. *Good. I hope that stung at least a little.* I picked up the infant from where she sat upon the bar and wrapped her up in her blanket again and held her close to me.

"Well, *she* is going to get grabbed up and sold into a lifetime of service to the Arch Authority unless we hide her away right now," said Sam, glancing around the room with fear shadowing her eyes.

"I'm sure you're right. That's how I ended up here, saving her from being nabbed by another Jules from Erde."

Gamma Jules' eyes widened. "What? From Erde? Are you sure? Because she's not with the Arch Authority. Erde staged an invasion of Arne through Arch Network portals years ago, and since then, the Arch Authority doesn't even have a base of operations there. Just a portal that's managed from Arne."

I furrowed my brow and tried to make soothing sounds at a fussy Lucy, wriggling and whistling in my embrace. "Really? Isn't one of the famous Dionnes in Erde?"

The other Jules shrugged. "Yes, but she's never been part of the Arch Network, either. The Arch people just built on her invention. Sure, they supply her with all the research money and materials she wants, but she doesn't work *for* them. She came out against the United States of Dixie's incursion, and it's even suspected that she helped cut off all portal access to Arne to strand the first wave of troops in Arne. Hasn't made her very popular on her homeworld, at least in the U.S. of D. Other factions there love her, though."

"Okay," said Sam. "I think we all agree that it would be bad for the Arch to grab little Lucy here. You're not okay with—er—Jules taking her away to be hidden. You have no idea even what *world* your precious Hope's Tour might be in at the moment. What *do* you want to do to protect her? You can't just keep running on your own, Jules. You need a plan. We'll help, but you've got to let us."

"Fine," I said. "Let's get help from Dionne. The one here on Beta."

Sam blinked. "Dionne Sutton? The Environmentalist? What's she going to do, make sure you use cloth diapers for Lucy?"

"What are you thinking? Maybe she's got connections with the other Dionnes, and maybe they might be able to get you past the Arch Authority's reach somehow?"

I nodded. "Something like that. Maybe she's got access to a private portal, or at least portal technology that's not controlled by Arch people."

Sam and Gamma Jules exchanged a look and shrugged. Sam said, "Well, it might work. But it's going to be a risk getting to her."

I smiled. "Why? They don't even know I'm here yet. I didn't exactly come through the Arch."

Gamma Jules narrowed his eyes. "What? How?"

I shook my head. "Given the circumstances, I think I'll keep my secrets for now."

Sam glared at me. "Oh, no. If you want our help, you're gonna spill.

I sighed and pulled out the portal gun. I aimed it at a space in the middle of the bar. I pulled the trigger. A portal failed to appear. A red light blinked on top of the gun. Which I took to mean, it was out of juice. I was well and truly stuck. "Well, my way here isn't working to get me back out."

Sam stared at the portal gun, even as I put it away. "It sounds like you've been running ever since you left me without saying goodbye. I don't think you're as safe as you think you are."

I sighed. "It's true, the Jules from Erde has managed to find me twice now, the second time on a world that's not on the Arch Network at all. So, I admit I don't know everything. But I think I have a lead, at least. But where do we even find Dionne?"

Gamma Jules shrugged. "Figured you knew."

Sam pulled out her smartphone and poked at it for a few minutes. "Looks like she's with the National Oceanic and Atmospheric Administration. She's working on that big Weather Machine project."

Gamma Jules laughed. "Really? A weather machine?"

"No, really," I replied. "It's not a literal single machine that controls the weather. It's a global effort to track weather patterns, intending to learn how to alter them. Nobody believed they'd be able to change the weather, but since the weather machine project started, climate change has slowed by ten percent. That's a lot for only a few years!"

He scoffed. "How do you know that's not just statistics being manipulated?"

"We don't," said Sam. "But there's been enough interest in the project that multinational corporations are throwing a *lot* of money at the project. That's something, at least."

I waved my hands to change the subject. "Anyway, so that's great, but where's Dionne?"

Sam squinted at the little screen in her hand and then she smiled, holding up the phone for the other Jules and me to see. "Look! She's on an aircraft carrier!"

On the screen, a honey-blonde woman with elegant features stood on the deck of an aircraft carrier, the wind blowing her hair all around her head. She wore a red rain slicker emblazoned with the NOAA logo. On the deck behind her stood a buoy the size of a small gazebo, loaded with instrumentation and antenna arrays. Dionne waved a hand toward the buoy and her mouth moved as she spoke.

I prompted Sam. "Turn up the sound, I want to hear what she's saying."

Sam obliged, and Dionne Sutton's pleasant voice spoke from the phone.

"...will be one of a thousand additional 'eyes and ears' of the Weather Machine, many of which have already been deployed by my team from the USS Constellation. Formerly mothballed, we brought the Constellation out of retirement for peacetime duty, and it's been our home for the past two months. We're headed south, and hope to visit the Antarctic within a month, but we have a lot of stops along the way, so that might prove overly optimistic. These floating stations are autonomous and solar-powered, so they can maintain position and relay data for decades if need be."

"Bad news," said Sam, frowning. "The post with this video's dated yesterday."

"Oh no!" I cried. "She's halfway around the world! Now, what can we do?"

"Maybe we could talk with her online? If she's posting videos, surely she's got a nice network connection, even out on the ocean. Here, I'll shoot her an email. What should I say?"

I bit my lower lip and thought awhile, then said, "Maybe don't *say* much, just send her a picture of Lucy."

"Are you nuts?" asked my doppelganger. "If that picture gets out, the Arch Authority will know you're in Beta. And they'll be after you, too, Sam, if it gets linked to your email account and phone."

"We have to trust someone," I said. "And Dionne's right up there among the best scientists, like Neil deGrasse Tyson. I feel like she and her alts are pretty well known for their altruistic projects. And what's the alternative? I can't just hide here, I don't know where or how to get back to Hope's Tour alone, and the Arch Authority or whoever Erde Jules is working for is gonna catch up with me eventually if I do nothing."

The three of us exchanged glances and nodded.

Lucy burped. She giggled, clicked, and squeaked.

"Say cheese," said Sam, holding up her phone. It made a clicking sound effect, and she showed me the picture. I would swear it looked like Lucy was mugging for the camera.

"It'll do," I said. "Tell her we're in trouble and need her help getting off-world discretely."

"What's this 'we' stuff?" asked Gamma Jules. "I left Gamma to get away from trouble. You ran away and found trouble."

I glared at him. "Forgive me for being a problem. I'll be out of your hair soon enough, one way or another. You're taking over my old life, I figure you owe me at least this much."

Sam made a show of clicking "send" on the email, then whirled on me. "No. You don't get to talk to him that way. He's picked up where you left off. If anything, you owe *him* for that, Jules."

My face flushed and my stomach knotted. "Is that how you see it? You still don't understand? That's fine. I'm sure your daddy will be happy to have a replacement for me that's more mainstream and respectable."

"Hey!" cried Gamma Jules. "I'm right here! You can't talk about me like that!"

"Buddy, I'm doing all I can to hold it together, and you're not making it any easier. Just help me out and you won't have to worry about me anymore. Okay?"

Sam's eyes lowered to stare at Lucy. "That's not fair, Jules. What else was I supposed to do? You gave up your right to be a part of my life when you ran off. It's probably best that you go as soon as you can. I don't think the two of you belong in the same place. If nothing else, it's creepy."

I turned around to look around the room, in part because I was afraid of her seeing the tears prickling at the corners of my eyes. All eyes were on the three of us, and that made me worry. "Can we take this somewhere more private?"

We walked a block together to a parking garage, where Sam let us in her SUV and drove us out of downtown. I knew where we'd end up, our apartment. My former home. Right now, I'd have preferred to be going almost anywhere else, but I didn't have any better ideas.

Please forgive me, I'm going to skim over some details here. The drive with my ex and my replacement lasted far longer than I wanted it to. Being there in the old place twisted my guts more than I anticipated. And I'll admit, a different kind of homesickness washed over me, and I second-guessed my hasty decision to go on the road more than once.

It was so difficult, I had to retreat into the bathroom to be alone for a while. But while I sat in there nursing my jealousy and regrets, something happened. Those hard emotions caught fire and burned like embers deep inside me.

I hadn't failed Sam. She'd failed me.

I might have run away from a bad situation, but she'd replaced me almost *immediately*.

The only regret I had when I emerged from the bathroom to face them again was regretting asking Sam for help. I hadn't asked to come back to my homeworld. I hadn't asked to be dumped there with no options. I hadn't even sought her out, at least not consciously.

I stalked out into the living room and snapped at Sam. "Let me use your phone. I think I made a mistake coming to you, Sam. I'll call Patrick, and you'll be done with me."

Sam and the other Jules turned to stare at me with wide eyes. Sam drew a breath and let it out. "What's all this?"

"I don't want to talk about it," I said, struggling to keep my anger under control. "Just let me use your phone, okay?"

Sam shook her head. "No. Spill. What's going on."

I gestured at Gamma Jules. "Look. You have every right to move on. I just didn't expect to be so easily replaced."

"Look, Jules," said Gamma Jules. "I didn't expect—"

Sam interrupted him, her face clouding with anger. "No, Jules. Let's have this out. You *left*."

I nodded. "Yes, and I don't blame you for being upset about that. We've been through this. You know my reasons. I wish I'd been able to handle it more kindly, but this isn't all on me. We, the both of us, had a problem. I walked because I wasn't being respected. I get that you don't see it that way. That's fine. So just let me borrow your phone, okay?"

Gamma Jules opened his mouth to speak, but Sam held up the flat of her hand in his direction to stop him, eyes still fixed on mine.

She said, "Jules, do you want this to end badly? Again?"

I took a deep breath and closed my eyes, then looked at her as I let it out. "I didn't want it to end at all. Not really. I still love you, Sam. I just couldn't stay, okay?"

Sam slumped a little, and something in her eyes melted. "I love you too, Jules. Why else would I replace you with—I mean, let's be real—with *you*?"

Gamma Jules spluttered. "I'm not them, I'm *me*!"

Sam sighed and gave him a long, sad, look. "Of course. But Jules has a point. You're already in my life as much as you are because you're so much like my—I mean, that—Jules.

His brow furrowed; his eyes narrowed. He looked away from her.

"Oh, you know what I mean!" Sam let out a frustrated noise.

Just then, Sam's laptop lit up and made a ringing sound.

"Oh!" she cried. "It's Dionne! She must have gotten my email!"

Sam glanced at me and the other Jules, then clicked the "answer" button. The larger-than-life face of Dionne Sutton appeared. Lines etched her face in ways I hadn't seen on the video earlier or her other public appearances. In particular, a vertical line of worry bisected her eyebrows. She swept long honey-colored bangs out of her face and tucked her hair behind an ear.

She seemed to see me and brightened a bit. "Jules! It is you! I'm really glad you and Sam reached out to me. If you're anything like your alts, you're just the person we need right now."

I blinked and put my newly stoked rage on a back burner for the moment. "Me? I'm nobody, just a roadie. A bartender."

Dionne's eyes widened and she shook her head. "If I've learned anything in dealing with my alts, it's that everyone's special, everyone's got their strengths. And no matter what differences there may between alts, there's a shared core between them, some essence that makes them similar enough to *be* alts, living different lives, but as each would if their roles were reversed. You two Jules in that room, you're individuals, special separately, but you're closer than family, closer than siblings."

Gamma Jules and I exchanged a long look. He cracked a little smile after a few breaths, and I found that I wore the same smile on my face. Not a mirror, but close.

"See?" said Sam, crossing her arms across her chest in vindication. "Different, but the same!"

"So?" I said to Dionne. "So what if I am special? What does someone like me have that you want? If anything, I need help from you."

As if on cue, Lucy let out a trilling whistle and a rather rude noise.

Dionne smiled and nodded. "I hope we can help each other. First, tell me where you got this little darling?"

"She fell into my lap on Theta Earth," I quipped.

The vertical line reappeared. "*Theta* Earth? I wasn't aware that there *was* an Earth called Theta."

I smiled and shrugged. "There is now. At least, that's what I'm calling it. Unless they'll let me call it Juleslandia. It's a world I found in a rip in space between Delta Earth and some unknown destination. She was already in the care of a friend's alt. It seems she arrived through the same rip, though I can't imagine how."

"I think your Delta alt may have the answer to that," said Dionne.

Some of my back-burner rage flowed back to the front. "What? Delta? No, no, no. Delta Jules sold us out to Arch Authority goons."

She shook her head. "I can't believe that. Delta Jules has been working with me and my alts to free the Tristellians the Arch Authority's been using to maintain their network."

Without thinking about it, I took a couple of steps toward the screen. "Wait. You *knew*? All you Dionnes knew? The wonderful, altruistic Dionnes knew about the inhuman treatment of these people? How could you let it happen?"

Dionne's eyes dropped and she shook as though the weight of the world rested upon her shoulders. In a weaker voice, she said, "Not at first. We assumed they'd used technology to solve the portal stability problem to allow for permanent links to be possible. But the more my alts from Alpha, Luna, and Erde worked on this, the more it pointed towards a more sinister truth. Even Alpha's Quantum-Turing computer at its best couldn't have held a portal open twenty-four-seven. Certainly not one big enough to drive a truck through. Our worst fears were confirmed when your Delta Jules contacted us and told us of Coral's plight. I want to personally thank you for freeing him."

I said, "I don't want to know someone who could have left him in that horrible pod, in disgusting conditions, in solitary confinement. I *had* to do something."

She raised her eyes and seemed to meet my gaze. "Not everyone would, or he wouldn't have been confined like that." She seemed to glance at Sam, and then back at me.

I had no reply to that, so I picked up Lucy and held her in my arms. She wriggled with delight and nuzzled my chin.

"Do you know that Delta is all but cut off right now, as a result?" said Dionne, her eyes deep and serious.

I snorted. "Yeah, I guess I kind of do know that. At least the Delta-to-Achse gate in Chicago is down."

"Wait," said Sam. "That was *you*? That's all over the news!"

I offered her a sheepish grin in response.

"So, do you still say you're nobody?" asked Dionne.

Again, I had no reply.

Dionne ran a hand through her hair but kept her eyes locked on mine. "You're a friend of Hope, aren't you, Jules?"

"Well, yes. She took me in, and we've gotten close." As Sam's eyes narrowed, I added, "I've gotten close with her whole crew. They treat me like family."

"Hope," said Dionne, "Is the key to all of this. She's the only known free Tristellian in Arch Authority space. My alts and I believe that she's only eluded capture because of her fame. We think that Hope and her crew could bring down the Arch Network. We think she can use her people's powers to free the others of her *original* crew that are enslaved by the Arch Authority. We need you to link back up with Hope's Tour and guide them to Erde, to meet with my alt there. She has technology that only Hope could use to accomplish this."

"But how?" I sighed. "I don't even know where Hope *is* right now, Dionne. I don't know how to get there, even if I did."

"I have connections," said Dionne. "But you hold the best connection in your arms."

"W-what?" I stammered. "Lucy? How?"

"All you need is a portal, a clear memory of Hope, and the little one can get you to her. And I've got the portal. Stand by."

Dionne stepped off-camera for a moment, and the walls of her room lit up with a crackling electrical light.

And then, right there in Sam's living room, blue arcs of electricity formed a small oval, which grew to be as large as the one that'd been at the foot of the bed only a few hours ago, shimmering like an upended pool of mercury.

Chapter 21 – Kind-Hearted Woman

I awoke to the smell of fishy flatulence. I lay on a flat, padded surface. The world around me bumped and jostled from side to side. Familiar voices, full of stress, fired back and forth at each other all around me. Lights flashed on the other side of my eyelids, and I let out a groan as unremembered pain shot through my limbs.

Opening my eyes, I beheld the source of the smell. Baby Lucy stood on all fours on my chest, giving me a toothy Tristellian grin. She whistled and giggled.

"Ugh, someone needs a poopy diaper change," I mumbled.

"Jules!" cried Babs, appearing in my view, behind the infant. "You're awake!"

As my bleary eyes focused on her, it came to me that she stood in the main cabin of *La Esperanza*, the massive tour bus for Hope's Tour.

I was home! But how?

I shook my head. "Since I don't know how I got here, I'm not certain that I *am* awake," I said, giving her a slight smile.

Marcy arrived at my side and shined a penlight in each of my eyes. "Good, you don't have a concussion. What's the last thing you remember?"

"Uh. I was back on Beta. With Sam. Talking to Dionne. The environmentalist Dionne of my world, I mean. She, uh, had just remotely opened a portal near me."

The delphine face of Hope appeared between Babs and Marcy. She said nothing, but her eyes widened as I looked back at her.

Marcy touched my forehead and then the side of my neck. "Jules, we found you and this baby Tristellian laying in the road ahead of us. As in, Zamboni had to slam on the brakes to keep from rolling over you both. Last we saw of you and—well—and the other Jules, you'd bailed out between worlds. How'd you even get to Beta? And who is Sam?"

An unseen Dribbler, somewhere behind the others, answered for me. "She's their fiancée."

I nodded. "My ex-fiancée. She and Gamma Jules were helping us—"

"*Gamma* Jules?!" exclaimed Dribbler.

"Yes," I replied. "It seems he's taken up my life where I left off. I got to Beta from Theta Earth—"

"*Theta* Earth?" asked a surprised Marcy.

I sighed. "I love you all, and I'm so glad to be back home, but would you *please* let me answer your questions before blurting out more?"

Marcy and Babs drew pinched fingers across their lips to show that they were zipped. Hope just showed me her pointed teeth in a silent grin.

Lucy let out a stream of clicks and imitated Hope's grin and let out another deadly baby fart.

I must have made a face because hands reached past Hope and scooped up the infant and pulled her elsewhere.

"Theta Earth," I began again, "is what I'm calling another Earth-like world where I ended up after I fell off of *La Esperanza* in the between-space outside of Delta. I met a *very* friendly double of Dribbler's, who had been caring for baby Lucy for a few weeks. When we made it back to his place, Erde Jules popped in, like she did back on Gamma, and tried to abduct the baby. I stopped her and used her portal gun to jump to Beta. It seems that the portals it makes send you to your homeworld. It only had the one shot in it, because it stopped working after the one shot."

Marcy bit her lip and exchanged looks with Babs and Hope. The three of them waited for me to continue, even though it was clear to me that they wanted to ask more questions.

"I think I stranded Erde Jules on Theta with Dribbler's twin. I hope they get along because the only way I know of to get in or out of there without a portal-generator is about thirty feet above a patch of Lake Michigan."

Marcy's mouth popped open into an "o" of surprise, but she waited to see if I was done.

"Anyway, that's all I know. Like I said, I haven't got a clue how I got here. For all I know, this is just a wonderful dream I'm having after stepping through Dionne's portal."

Somewhere towards the rear of the bus, Dribbler let out a disgusted cry and complained about poopy alien diapers.

Hope broke her silence. "Jules my love, do you remember stepping through that portal?"

"No, I—wait—maybe? It's fuzzy, like a dream, but I remember Dionne asked me to do something, and I agreed. Sam didn't want me to do it, for some reason."

Hope touched my hand with hers. A cool wave washed over me, and my memories came into greater focus. "Hmm, Dionne—I can almost remember it now, it's not the tip of my tongue—she said we have to get you to Erde. She said you were the only one who could bring down the Arch network and save your people. And she said her counterpart in that world could help you. Us, I mean."

"Us," said Hope, her grin fading. With a sad tone to her voice, she sang, "Do you think I'd be okay putting you in that kind of danger, Jules? You or the rest of my Hope's Tour family?"

"Do you think you could stop *us* from helping?" I said with a smile.

Babs and Marcy nodded their agreement with that.

Before Hope could protest, I blurted out, "Do you know what happened to Delta Jules? I left them behind in the tunnel, under fire. I had no choice, they attacked me on top of *La Esperanza*, and I had to get away. But Dionne told me that Delta Jules has been working with the other Dionnes to free Tristellians, like Coral. Come to think of it, I wonder if that's how Lucy ended up on Theta? If we're on the same side, why would they attack me? It makes no sense!"

Marcy sighed. "I don't think we should trust Delta Jules based just on what Dionne says. Genius or no, she might not know what's going on any more than we do."

I stared at her. "Then what do we do? If Dionne is wrong, then maybe she's wrong about her counterpart on Erde as well. Do we trust her to go right to the center of the web? Remember, Erde Jules keeps coming after us. And someone's been trying to get Hope killed."

"Well, that's the Arch Authority," said Babs.

I sat up, to face them. "Seems likely. If Jules is a double-agent, are they playing Arch Authority stooge while doing work for the Dionnes, or is it the other way around? What's their motivation? They were *angry* at me when I followed them up top."

Marcy shook her head. "To answer your question, we were too busy dodging gunfire to pay attention to what happened to Delta Jules. Maybe they were captured or reclaimed by the Arch Authority? Maybe they found their own wormhole to slip down after you disappeared? I hate to suggest it, but maybe they're dead?"

I thought about that for a moment, then shook my head. "I feel like we're going to see them again before this is all over."

Hope nodded and sang, "I have that feeling too."

I looked around the room. "Hey, what happened to Harlan? And how *did* you all get away from that Arch Authority mini-tank?"

Babs put a hand on my shoulder and spoke in a soft voice. "Harlan's in bad shape, *chica*. He took a shot in his left arm pretty bad."

Hope lowered her muzzle and her eyes shone brightly as she sang, "I did what I could, but I couldn't save the arm."

Dribbler re-entered the main cabin, cradling a wiggly baby Lucy in his arms. "You did good, Hope. He's gonna live, you know?"

Marcy sat down next to me and said, "I wish he hadn't resorted to heroics. He had a couple of Dixie grenades left in his pack, so he got back up top to try to scare off the Arch Authority goons. Grenades ended up disabling the mini-tank, but they shot him as he threw the second one."

Babs touched my chin and held my eyes with hers. "Harlan thought the other Jules had killed you, sweetie. For him, it was revenge, and a chance for the rest of us to escape."

Tears stung my eyes, and I wiped at them with the back of my hand. "Oh no. Oh, Harlan! I'm so sorry!"

Babs lifted my chin and brought her face very close to mine. "No. Do not do this. Harlan is a soldier. Weeping for him does him no honor. He has faced enough dishonor in the past, do not cast his heroic actions as a tragedy, Jules."

"But if I hadn't—"

Marcy interrupted me. "Stop it. That's not productive. What you did up there, with the smoke bombs, it bought us time. You fought for us just as valiantly as Harlan. And he's going to be fine!"

Hope drew a deep breath and let it out with whistles and clicks that delighted Lucy. Then, she sang, "Harlan will be up and barking orders in no time. I, too, did my best. The time for regrets is over. Let us be more productive and plan our next steps! But first, Jules, it is critical to know, how did Beta Dionne know how to send you to us? Does she have a way to track us?"

Marcy's eyes looked haunted at this suggestion.

I shook my head. "That's not it. My memory is still fuzzy, but I think Lucy brought us here."

Hope glanced from me to the baby, and back again. "How is this possible?"

I spread my hands before me. "I don't fully understand it, but Dionne said it had to do with why the Arch Authority needs your people to maintain its fixed Arch gates between worlds. You have a meta-connection to the multiverse. Your minds aren't set in a single reality, but span possibilities. What happened with Coral makes more sense now, he was able to use the gate to send him wherever he wanted, while I just appeared on the other side."

Hope shook her head. "I do understand what you're saying, but it is not quite wherever. It is within a certain—ah—distance. All of the Earths in the Arch Network are very close, in meta-space, for example, but Erde and Arne and others in the extended network are a bit further. So, that portal gun allowed you to go to your homeworld in a blink, and Coral is likely in some other Earth nearby, but you and little Lucy have jumped much further than this."

I glanced out the window and saw only the dark of night. "Really? Where are we, then?"

"We are on a world called League," said Marcy. "We've been through here before. It's on the other side of Achse. The experimental gate we went through took us further than any Arch gate should be able to. This is good for us, but possibly a bad sign overall; it suggests that the Arch Network is about to take a leap in technology and double their reach."

I blinked at her. "Why is that bad?"

Marcy glanced at Lucy, who still wriggled in Dribbler's arms. "They're gonna need more Tristellians."

"Oh no," I said, feeling the weight of the worlds settle upon my shoulders.

"My point is," sang Hope, "either there was something special about Beta Dionne's gate, or that baby can do things that even I can not. Maybe she just does not know her limits, and therefore is not so limited as her elders?"

I shrugged. "I don't know. Dionne had faith in her to get me to you. I don't know how, since she's never met you, and I didn't have any idea where you might be. Certainly, I've never been to League before. All I remember about them is that they have a world government and have a colony on Mars?"

Hope nodded. "Yes, they are advanced in many physical technologies, but their computers are not as powerful as your world, or those of Delta. I know of only one other world where humans have extra-terrestrial colonies. League is peaceful and ambitious."

Dribbler added, "They love our music, too, so they're clearly quite civilized."

Babs snorted. "You call your drumming civilized? *Chico*, you have the savage beats that get the crowd's juices flowing!"

They exchanged a playful grin, and I felt warm inside for the first time since waking up.

"Hope," I asked, "how far away is Erde from here?"

She looked me in the eyes and smiled. "Just on the other side of Arne, love."

I thought a moment. "I remember Harlan saying that Arne cut Erde off from the Arch Network when the United States of Dixie tried to invade them. I feel like that means there's one of your kin being held captive there."

Hope nodded. "It would seem that way."

I smiled. "What do you say to a little rescue mission along our way?"

The faces around me lit up, so I knew their answer without a word.

"Okay, then. First thing we need to do is to plan a concert in Arne."

Marcy grinned. "I can arrange that."

Babs held up her hands. "Wait. Wait. We need to get to Erde Dionne. The Arch Authority is hot on our heels. And you just want to *announce* where we're gonna be?"

I nodded. "We're safer in plain sight. They know we're dangerous to them, but it'll be a really bad look to have us killed or captured in public. And what's more public than a concert? Not to mention, we're going to need a cover story."

Babs smiled. "You're my kind of crazy, Jules. Let's do it!"

Chapter 22 – Terraplane Blues

"There's just one problem with my plan," I said. "We need to go through an Arch portal to get from League to Arne."

"*One* problem?" cried Babs. "*Chica*, I can think of a *bunch* of problems! How are we gonna bust a captive Tristellian out of the Arch facility? How do we even know where they're kept? After you freed Coral on Delta, they're gonna be watching for just such a stunt, aren't they?"

Hope sang soothing words. "Let us work on one problem at a time, and we will figure it out.

Dribbler sat down next to me, baby Lucy in his arms. "Jules, you probably don't know it, but we can travel kinda incognito. *La Esperanza* has smart paint from Alpha Earth that lets us change its appearance. And Marcy has connections. Don't you, *Miz* Davenport?"

Marcy grinned. "That I do. I'll go up front to have Zamboni change the exterior to look like a tourist bus, and I'll see what strings I can pull."

Babs put her hands upon her hips. "So, what about the other big problem?"

I shrugged. "That depends. What do we know about Arne's Arch Authority? Do they have a Jules of their own?"

Babs, Dribbler, and Hope all exchanged blank looks and shook their heads.

Hope sang, "We really don't know. I have not heard such. But I did not know about Delta Jules, either. Your doubles do seem to be at the center of things, my love, so I would not doubt it. We are no longer in the realm of Earths, though, so your double here might not be as much like you as the ones you've met so far. There might not be a Jules analogue here at all."

Dribbler spoke up. "There's a Jules *and* a Dionne in Erde, and that's even further than League or Arne from the Earths."

Hope smiled. "Yes, we are still not very far away, which is why I would not be surprised to find another Jules there."

I sighed. "But would they be an ally? Delta Jules is pretty sketchy, and Erde Jules has been downright nasty."

"No one can know that, love," sang Hope. "But either way, it might buy you a way into the Arch."

I shook my head. "I get that, but without a virtual map like Delta Jules gave me, I won't know where to go."

Hope touched her snout with her hand. "Perhaps not," she sang, "but I might. I believe I might be able to sense one of my kind if I were close to them."

"So, are we having the concert before, or after the rescue attempt?" asked Babs.

Hope grinned. "We will have them at the same time!"

I laughed. "Come on. How can we have a show if you're helping find another Tristellian elsewhere?"

She touched my hand with hers and looked into my eyes. "May I share myself with you? Will you share yourself with me, Jules?"

Not knowing what she meant, I decided to trust her and nodded.

The room blurred, like having my eyes crossed. In one split view of the room, I saw Hope and Babs standing behind her.

In the other, I saw myself, eyes wide, with Dribbler and Lucy nearby. Colors seemed muted, but I could tell exactly how far away everything in the room was, a sort of mapping superimposed upon what I could see. If I focused harder on Hope's view of the world, I realized the "map" refreshed every few seconds and depended upon sounds she made outside of my hearing range. *This must be what echolocation feels like!*

Lucy in particular stood out in sharp detail. I decided it must be due to her own ultra-high-pitched pings of echolocation. It had the eerie effect of making the humans in the room seem just a little less real.

Inside my head, Hope's voice sang. *Now you see and hear what I do, and I experience the world as you!*

In reply, I directed thoughts at her. *I didn't know you could do this!*

She grinned. *There is much about each other that remains to be discovered!* Out loud, she sang, "Jules and I are linked."

"Oh," said Babs. "You mean, like that one time—with me—?"

Hope nodded, making me feel strange as I both watched her do it, and felt her doing it. "Yes. We are not one and the same, but we share our perceptions and surface thoughts. If we were on Delta, this same thing could be accomplished with cross-feeds on Specs. But it is an innate thing my people can do, sharing our realities."

I spoke, a little unnerved by hearing my voice from my own ears and also from Hope's. "H-how long can you keep this up? And what limits does it have?"

Hope let go of my hand and my perceptions snapped back into my head, my senses no longer split. She sang, "We may stay linked for a little over an hour, so long as both of us may spare some attention for the link. Once the link is broken, we would have to touch again to re-establish it. You will find that it is tiring to maintain. But I believe that in this way, I may be with you even as I perform."

I stared at her a long moment. "Hope? What's the plan? Will I infiltrate alone?"

Hope shook her head. "No. Babs at least should go with you."

Dribbler perked up. "Me too, right? They might need my help."

"No, dear Dribbler. I will need you with me, especially if our Harlan is still recovering. We will be spread thin. Marcy is going to have to be the entire crew. Lucy will need to stay on *La Esperanza* with Zamboni, for safety."

I frowned. "How will the two of you perform without Babs?"

Hope grinned. Babs sighed and laughed.

I filled in the blank for myself. "Gotcha. The show must go on, right?"

"Yes, Jules. It will be billed as an 'unplugged' show. We will figure out the details once we are safely in Arne."

Babs snorted. "Safely. Those people stopped an invasion dead. They're ruthless."

Dribbler laughed. "Maybe. But Erde burned Arne's Baltimore to the ground before the Arch Authority managed to close the gate."

"It was a massacre." Harlan growled as he descended the spiral steps one at a time. "Arne people seem civilized, but they'll fight like savages if you push 'em. Doubt Dixie could have taken over even if they'd kept the lines open. We just didn't know what we got ourselves into. Guess it seemed like a good idea to someone higher up at the time. Like as not, someone high up enough to sit at a desk back in Richmond, maybe. They didn't want to spare me, but they've got rules, and savage or no, when a man lays down his arms and surrenders? Well, I'm here today anyway. Can't say I want to go back to visit, but you know me. Crazy plan or not, I'm in."

Harlan clung to the rail of the stair as he stood at the bottom, and I couldn't tell you whether his face held a grin or a grimace. I marveled at his being upright only days after losing most of his arm. I leaped from my seat to help him, but he waved me off with a stubborn grunt.

Jasmine slunk down the stairs and rubbed against Harlan's legs. The cat's eyes were huge and she held her ears flat out to either side.

"No, Harlan dear," sang Hope. "You have much healing to do. You should be in your cabin!"

"I can't just sit by!" he protested. "I'll work the sound and lights, since you're sendin' Jules off on another damn fool errand."

I smiled. "Seems that's playing to my strengths."

He looked me in the eye and pressed his lips into a flat line. "Good to see you in one piece. Thought we lost ya."

"I wish I could say the same for you. I'm really sor—"

Harlan snarled. "Don't you *dare* finish that sentence. You did what I told you to do, and you got ambushed. I don't know what that other Jules was up to, but my gut says it were nothin' good. I figure you saved us from somethin' nastier."

"But Delta Jules is working with the Dionnes! They're supposed to be on our side! Why did they attack me?"

Harlan grunted. "You think I know? I'm as flummoxed as anyone about that."

Hope interrupted us. "I do not believe you are healed enough to be up and around, Harlan!"

The glint in Harlan's eyes told me as much as the note of desperation in his voice. "Ma'am, with all due respect, your high-tech healing disk has me patched up good enough for now. I'm not gonna be a hundred percent, but I gotta help out somehow. Please."

The two of them stared at each other for a long moment. Too long. The tension in the cabin stretched to breaking.

I had to do something.

"Harlan?" I said, pulling out the portal gun. "This is from your world; it creates very temporary portals. Do you know enough about Erde tech to get it working again? It would come in handy for our rescue attempt."

Harlan harumphed. "I don't know nothin' about portal technology."

I held it out toward him. "I don't think it's broken. I think it's just out of juice. Think you could figure out how to charge it?"

The stage manager didn't hesitate. He took two steps toward me and took the portal gun and grasped it in his hand like a weapon, sighting down the fluted barrel, muzzle aimed at the floor. "Maybe. If it's got one of them Sutton batteries, maybe we could charge 'er up. I'll see what I can do. Thanks."

Hope took a step toward Harlan, then stopped. She watched him a moment, then caught my gaze in hers, eyes smoldering with something fierce but secret. She sang, "If you must."

Marcy burst into the room. "We're a League tourist excursion! Hope, you need to make the baby and yourself scarce in case we get searched. Everyone else, get ready, we're headed for the Arch portal to Arne! Ohmigod, Harlan, you're up!"

Harlan scrunched his face into a scowl and set the portal gun down on a seat and rummaged around in the overhead compartment, coming up with a toolbox. As he placed it next to the portal gun, I noticed his face turning deeper and deeper red, a glimmer of wetness filling the weathered wrinkles around his eyes.

I lowered my voice so that only Harlan could hear. "You know, it's okay to ask for help."

He wouldn't meet my eyes. "Maybe for you. Maybe on a good day. But not today. I gotta soldier on. It's important. But I appreciate what you already done for me, understand?"

I drew breath and said in as soft a tone as I could, "Okay. Just don't soldier on past your limits. No matter what Hope says, we're going to need everyone to pull this off. Understand?"

He grunted, but his head bobbed in a barely perceptible nod. He sifted through the contents of the toolbox, pulling out a meter, a soldering iron, and some electrical tape.

Jasmine bumped up against my shins and chittered at me. I reached down and scratched her between the ears, murmuring. "What's up, girl?"

The cat nipped my hand and then leaped up on a seat and pawed at the window.

I peered out to see what she wanted. Outside, the orderly lights of the nighttime city flowed past, and all seemed well.

But then I noticed a blue, flashing light illuminating the buildings and vehicles we passed. It reminded me of a strobe light. But why would there be a strobe following us? And why would it be getting brighter? It was like—

I called out toward the driver's compartment. "Zamboni! I think we've got someone on our tail!"

The robot's voice crackled and buzzed over the main cabin intercom. "Arch Authority vehicles closing in. Awaiting orders."

Marcy turned and threw herself into the driver's compartment, and I could hear her shouting at Zamboni. Dribbler dashed toward the rear of the bus, past the kitchenette and on into the cargo area. Hope's feet disappeared up the stairs to the bunk compartments. Harlan remained hunched over the portal gun, prodding it with the probes of the meter, face twisted into a pained scowl.

Lost in indecision, I asked him, "Harlan, what should I do?"

He raised his eyes to meet mine. "Better decide who you are, kiddo, then get ready to bullshit. 'Cause if they board us, you're gonna have to think fast.

Not knowing what to do with Harlan's advice, I rushed up to join Marcy and Zamboni in the forward compartment. "How close are we to the Arch?"

Marcy started to answer, but Zamboni interrupted. "We are seven hundred and eighty-two meters from the Arch Gate."

"Floor it, Zamboni," I said, gripping the back of Marcy's chair.

Zamboni complied before Marcy could object. The bus thrashed from side to side, dodging around other cars and trucks with inhuman precision. Streetlights and the signs upon buildings flashed past, and my breath left me as we scraped past traffic as though we were in the middle of some kind of very important, very dangerous video game.

Sirens wailed behind us, strobing blue lights reflecting off of every surface surrounding *La Esperanza* in her mad flight through the city.

Marcy and I screamed in harmony as Zamboni piloted the massive bus into oncoming traffic and across the well-lit, flag-bedecked courtyard in front of the stone and glass structure of the Arch Authority building. A couple dozen people scattered out of our path as we barreled toward the gaping silvery maw of the Arch Gate. Our reflection rushed towards us at a mad, impossible rate, and I swear I saw my own saucer eyes in the window just before we plunged into the space between the worlds.

Except, something went very wrong. Instead of the swirling colors and surreality of the between space, we emerged in an instant on the other side of the Arch, blue lights still flashing all around us, accompanied by the wail of sirens.

Marcy and I screamed in unison once more as Zamboni dodged the vehicles suddenly facing us on the other side of the now-dead Arch gate.

Dribbler called out from the main cabin. "What the hell happened?"

"We're in trouble!" I cried. "The gate switched off! We're still in League!"

I left Marcy barking orders to Zamboni to evade the Arch Authority cruisers closing in on us. The robot turned the wheel and slammed on the brake and then hit the gas, propelling the tour bus back into city traffic. Blue lights flashed, reflected in every car window and lighting up the face of every building that we passed. Horns blared in our wake, and tires screeched.

I emerged into the main cabin to find Harlan throwing down his tools in frustration. "Damn it all! No point in fixin' this dang thing if we're just gonna get arrested. Arch thugs would *love* to get their hands on this gadget. I figure we better destroy it so they can't get ahold of it!"

He came up with a hammer and put the partially disassembled portal gun on the floor.

"Wait, Harlan, no!" I cried.

Dribbler reached out and stopped Harlan from swinging the hammer. "Whatcha got in mind, dude?"

I looked wildly around the cabin for ideas. "Harlan, can you power that thing directly?"

Harlan stared at me like I had asked if he had a spare pineapple in his pocket. "Huh? What, you think we can just plug 'er into the wall or somethin'? Maybe. Even if we did, how are we gonna fit the whole bus through a portal the size this thing makes? Even with a month to tinker with it, I wouldn't know how to change how it works that way!"

I shook my head. "Look, the only way we're getting out of this is in handcuffs, or by abandoning the bus. If you can power that directly somehow, we'll make a portal right here and we'll all jump through."

Dribbler almost sobbed as he said, "Leave *La Esperanza*? Dude, she's like a part of the family!"

"There's no other way, Dribbler! Maybe we'll get her out of impound later, but if we don't get Hope and Lucy out of here at least, they'll end up enslaved by the Arch Authority!"

Harlan's eyes flashed hot anger. "Right. Dribbler, help me pry up that deck plate there, it has access to the power plant."

"But—"

"Damn it! Just do what I say, Dribs! Choosin' between Hope and the bus ain't a choice, and you know it!"

As if on cue, Hope descended the stair, baby Lucy in her arms. Her singing voice quavered. "We are escaping through a portal? To where loves?"

"If I understand it right, it depends on who fires the portal gun," I said. "It aligns with your quantum signature and sends you there."

"Then I must not be first," said Hope. "Even if it had the range, which it will not, my world was destroyed ten years ago. It is what my 'verseship was fleeing, the multidimensional implosion of Tristel."

"I don't think there's much safety on my Beta Earth," I said.

Dribbler looked up from assisting Harlan. "Not Gamma, neither."

Hope shook her head. "No Arch-controlled world would be a good idea. We must go onward to Harlan's homeworld as planned."

"Erde? Are you crazy?" called Harlan. A sudden fat electrical spark lit his face from below, even as the lights blinked off and on again and the engine hesitated.

"They have no love for the Arch Authority," sang Hope. "And our mission is to reach the Dionne of your world."

"I think it's our best shot," I said, wishing there was something I could do. "I don't know that we should be moving when we make the portal. I don't know if it would stick in place relative to the bus, or the position above the ground where it was summoned. If it's the latter, it'll just get dragged out of the bus, and I don't want to take that risk."

"So, what, you think we gotta *stop*?" asked Dribbler, handing a pair of cables to Harlan.

I nodded. "When you're ready."

Harlan grumbled. "You know we're gonna get boarded right after we stop, right?"

Shrugging, I said, "Do you have another idea?"

He stripped a wire with his teeth and spat as he twisted it around a terminal on the gun. "Nope. But we're gonna need time to get through the portal. And it don't stay open long, as I recall. Might have enough time for Hope and a couple others to hustle through, if someone stalls the Arch goons. Since I'm not much other use, I'll stay behind."

We all had to hold on as the bus careened around another corner. Marcy appeared in the doorway, listening to the conversation.

"I think you have to go through, I said, running my fingers through my hair as my thoughts raced. "I'm not sure enough that it's enough for you to fire the portal gun. You might have to be first through, too."

Harlan spat out another bit of wire insulation. "Well, damn it all. Me, Hope, and Lucy, then. Jasmine if I carry her. We'd need to buy more damn time once we're stopped."

"I'll bullshit them for a bit," said Marcy. "I'll dazzle them with bureaucratic nonsense while the rest of you jump through to Erde."

Hope clicked and whistled, and little Lucy imitated her. Hope sang, "Marcy, that is very brave, but we do not leave anyone behind."

Marcy laughed. "Don't worry about me, I've got connections to get me out of trouble soon enough, and I'll hook up with you all later. I'll even take care of *La Esperanza*, assuming Zamboni leaves her in one piece. Tell you what, if there's time, I'll just be the last through the portal, okay?"

Hope made no reply, her expression flat and unreadable.

Over the intercom, Zamboni spoke. "We are approaching a blockade. I am out of options for escape. Awaiting instructions."

I looked at our stage manager, fumbling with the portal gun, a coil of cabling stretching from the device into the open hatch. "Harlan?"

"I think it'll work. Anytime now."

I called out to the forward compartment. "Bring us to a stop, Zamboni, and come on into the main cabin when you've done that."

The bus shuddered as it came to a halt and Marcy made her way past the rest of us to hang onto the rail next to the hatch door. Zamboni the robot appeared in the doorway. Dribbler put his arm around me as he got in line.

There came a pounding on the hatch.

"You're sure, Marcy?" I asked.

She nodded and pressed the button to open it.

"Now, Harlan," I said.

Harlan faced away from all of us. He raised the portal gun and fired toward the front of the cabin, and a shimmering oval appeared.

"Go, go, go!" cried Dribbler.

Harlan stepped through and vanished.

Hope took a look over her shoulder, then followed him into the portal, still carrying Lucy. Jasmine darted after them.

I heard Marcy cry out as two bulky Arch troopers burst into the cabin, the intense beams of flashlights attached to their guns' long barrels sweeping the room.

Babs leaped across the room and dropped one of the guards with a full-body kick to his head.

Marcy cried out a belated, "Babs, no!" as a bloody spot bloomed on Babs' shoulder, knocking her to the floor.

A metallic blur crossed my vision as Zamboni rolled to interpose his body to block the troopers' view of the portal, Dribbler, and me. The robot used his third arm to shove Dribbler into me, and we both fell back into the portal.

The last thing I saw before the scene in *La Esperanza* vanished was Zamboni falling to the floor in a hail of gunfire.

Dribbler and I clung together as we fell—or maybe floated—in the center of a starry field that spun end over end around us. I tried to track the individual points of light and found that most had visible discs, like very small moons or relatively close planets. The light that emanated from each one of the points of light seemed to flicker and change with colors and motion, like a tiny peephole into a movie theater beyond the blackness of night.

Even stranger, when I looked directly at one of the dots of light, it seemed to me that I could hear voices coming from them. Some of them cried out in anguish. One even filled my head with a squeal and a stream of rapid clicks, and I had the terrible image of a Tristellian in despair. *Please, don't be my Hope!*

"What the actual *fuck*!" cried Dribbler, his mouth far too close to my ear.

"Just hold on," I said, doing my best to get ahold of my emotions. "Try to keep your thoughts calm. I think we want to just let this happen, at least if we want to end up where the others went."

"I thought we were goin' to Erde?"

"Yeah. But the portal gun is weird. Last time I was in a funky tube-like passageway. I guess this is different. I think we're surrounded by places. Possibilities."

He wriggled to try to get a look around in different directions as we spun. "But what if this is wrong, Jules? Where will we end up?"

I sighed and hugged him close to me. "I don't know. Our best shot is to let the portal carry us where it will, which should be Erde. Unless I'm wrong."

"Unless you're wrong! Well, what if you're wrong?"

I held him at arm's length to look in his eyes. "In that case, let me apologize in advance. I did my best to save us all. If I screwed up, well, I'm sorry, Dribs."

He looked at me, eyes searching me for something, then pulled me in very close. "May I kiss you?"

I answered by kissing him instead. I closed my eyes this time, so I could shut out the spinning universe around us, to make my world narrow just to the two of us. If we ended up lost between the worlds, at least we had this.

I liked kissing Dribbler. I could tell he needed me at this moment as much as I needed him. Time didn't matter while we embraced. That we floated or fell didn't matter, I couldn't feel motion of any kind. The past fell away, the future rushed up, there in that nowhere space and time. We were all that existed, all that mattered.

And then, a breeze caught my clothing and hair; a zephyr so faint that I almost dismissed it as imagination. I opened my eyes as Dribbler withdrew from the kiss with a dreamy expression.

His eyes widened to show their whites. He gasped, "Jules—"

I turned my head to see that one of the dots of light had grown to be a rabbit hole in space, with daylight pouring through. No, it was more like a manhole cover full of sunshine. But now it grew large as a child's wading pool, sunlight bathing our faces as we tumbled end over end toward it.

"Hang on!" I shouted as we fell into the hole and out into the air.

I braced myself for a fall, and we rolled together in grass, landing flat on our backs, side by side.

In unison, Dribbler and I burst out laughing until our sides hurt, glad to be alive and unhurt.

Something eclipsed the sun as it flew by. It chattered and rumbled as it disappeared over the hill upon which we lay.

We stopped laughing in an instant. I sat up and scanned the grassy hillside for cover or sign of the others. A crumbled road made of more cracks than pavement meandered past the base of the hill as if in no hurry to get anywhere soon.

"Jules, that was a helicopter! I thought Erde was like Victorian or somethin'?"

I crouched and peered each way down the road. I spied a few clusters of trees, but the area around us seemed to be flat farmland punctuated by occasional long, low hills.

"More like Jules Verne or H.G. Wells if I remember right. You didn't see the babayaga my counterpart from Erde drove. They have strange steampunk-like technology there. Hopefully, though, *this* is Erde. Come on, we have to get out of sight and find the others!"

I took his hand and pulled him up. We ran down toward the road, where we dashed for a stand of trees.

Just like a nightmare, we seemed to move in slow motion as the chopping of helicopter blades returned, and the shadow of the double-turbine, bubble-shaped craft swung around the hill and bore down upon us.

Gunfire ricocheted off the ground as the helicopter strafed the ground on either side of the road. It had struck so close that I knew it couldn't be an accident that they missed. I grabbed Dribbler and turned to face the war machine and raised my hands. I could see now that it bore a flag that parodied that of the United States I grew up in, except it had fewer stripes and a circle of fewer stars upon the field of blue in its upper corner.

"U.S. of Dixie, I presume," I said, trying to contain utter panic.
Dribbler followed my example and said, "Now what?"
I said, "We surrender. We can't outrun that thing."
"What about the others?"
"We can hope they escaped. Maybe we'll buy them time."

You know, it wasn't the first time I'd landed in jail. It was just my first time in another dimension.

And you know, I kind of knew that my first visitor in jail would be me. I just wasn't sure which me that might be.

"Hello Jules," said my double from Erde. She stood on the other side of the bars, wearing a navy blue, no-nonsense, full-skirted dress. She looked no worse for the wear of having been marooned in Theta for a day. She leaned on a folded parasol of the same color as she gazed at me with cold eyes.

I should have guessed.

"What do you want?" I asked, not rising from the hard bunk of my dank cell.

She smiled. "Is that any way to greet your sister?"

"You're not my sister. You're not even me. I'd never try to murder people like you have. I'd never resort to kidnapping babies."

She arched an eyebrow at me. "Would you not? You made off with that baby Tristellian easily enough. But you're right. We are not the same. You have not experienced the kind of loss I have. You have drifted through life without passion, Jules. You don't know what it is to be a part of something bigger than yourself. Not like I do."

Now I did stand, to look her in the eye. "Really? I'm curious. What could drive someone like me to go to the lengths you have?"

Her eyes flattened and her jaw set as she fixed me with an icy glare. "My father. He was a Dixie soldier. Part of the Arne liberation force. He died for his country, cut off by the actions of the formerly impartial Arch Authority. Left to die on alien soil."

I swallowed the nasty retort I'd prepared to throw back at her and said, "I'm sorry for your loss. My father left my mother when I was young. I didn't really know him. For what it might be worth, I envy you having gotten to know him at all."

Her lip curled into a sneer and she said, "I do not think you would trade places with me, if you went through what I have been through."

I sighed and shook my head. "I suppose I wouldn't. Fine. Whatever. Did you come to see me only to tell me how much worse you have it than me?"

"I came to see what you might tell me in order to gain your freedom. Where is the Tristellian and the child?"

I snorted. "I couldn't tell you even if I wanted to. We used your fancy portal gun to get here, but Dribbler and I didn't see anyone else when we arrived. Maybe they fell through to a different world?"

She studied me. "You're telling the truth. Or you think you are."

I shrugged. "Can't fool myself, can I?"

She turned and dismissed me with a wave and took a couple of steps to leave.

I called after her. "Hey, wait! Where's Dribbler? What's going to happen to us?"

She glanced over her shoulder. "You'll be held here until we have no further use for you."

I needed more to go on. "How'd you even get out of Theta Earth after I left there? Did you go hang gliding over the lake?"

Her eyes narrowed. "You are not the only one with secrets and tricks. Dixie has more resources than you know."

"I know jack about Dixie, other than that a good friend of mine comes from there."

She smiled. "Ah yes. Your good friend, Mister Harper. Such a good friend to me, too. He gave me your itinerary. How else do you think I found you so easily?"

I must have gaped like a fool, because Erde Jules laughed at me, her eyes still narrowed.

She said, "Poor naïve Beta Jules. You take so much at face value. Like 'Delta Jules'. That was me! I arrived in Delta after you took the local Jules' Specs and went on your rescue mission. I disposed of that one to take their place at the theater, hoping to get you to spill what you did with Coral. That, or get a moment alone with Hope, to abuse her trust in you to do away with her. I did get to press Harlan for more intel on my way out, at least."

Her words knocked the wind out of me, and all I could do was shake my head in disbelief.

She laughed again and blew me a kiss. "Fare well, Jules. I do not think we shall meet again."

I watched, speechless, as she swept away down the hall. A door creaked open and then shut again with a final sort of clang.

I slumped back down upon my bunk for I don't know how long, thoughts swirling within my head like an aching whirlpool.

"Jules!" came a hissed voice from nearby.

I sat up. "Dribbler? Where are you?"

"Next cell over! I heard everything. What an evil bitch! I'm glad you're not—"

"Listen, Dribs, I'd really rather not talk about it. Got any ideas what happened to the others? Or a way out of here? Because I could really use some hope right now."

"Amen to that. Hope is something we both need."

"Some*one*, too," I added.

"Yeah. I feel like she'd know what to do, but I sure don't."

The door creaked open again, and another familiar voice reached my ears.

"Lazy, good for nothin'. Jes' sittin' around on yer butts while trouble's brewin'." Harlan stood before us, grinning, wearing what I realized must be a military uniform of the United States of Dixie.

I leaped to my feet and grasped the bars. "Harlan!"

"You double-crossing traitor!" growled Dribbler from next door.

Harlan held up his hands, palms toward us, as if to push back our words. "Now jes hold on now, gents. We got us a situation, there's no doubt about that. And it looks bad, I know."

"A little bird just told me you sold us out," I said. "Is it true?"

Harlan slumped and wouldn't meet my eyes. "Yeah. It's true. Or it was! But it isn't anymore! It wasn't supposed to go like that."

I heard Dribbler rattle the bars of his cell. "What was it *supposed* to go like, you fucker? Maybe you'd get a chance to sneak up to Hope's room and slit her throat? Maybe strangle her with sound cables?"

"No," he whispered. "No, I was just a spy. I needed to find out what I could about Tristellians, and why the Arch needed 'em. Hired on with Hope a couple years ago as a bodyguard, learned the ropes of runnin' the stage, and became part of the family."

"Family!" I cried. "What kind of family gives information to people who hunt their kin?"

He held up his hands again. "No, nothing like that. At least, I didn't know nothin' about killin' anyone. We were freedom fighters. Tryin' to take down the empire the Arch was buildin', so they couldn't oppress us or other worlds no more. No one told me Hope would be in danger. Like both of you, I fell for her hard. I'd do anything to protect her. I *did* protect her. When the handoff turned out to be an attempted bombing, and when your twin from here showed up to assassinate Hope, I did everything I could to protect her. And the rest of the family. Please believe me."

He reached up brush his fingers across the shortened sleeve of his uniform and what was left of his other arm.

"If that's so," I said between my teeth, "Why are you on that side of the bars?"

Harlan smiled. "Because they think I'm still on their side."

"But—" Dribbler was cut off as Harlan reached into a pocket and brought out a small handheld two-way radio that looked like it was from Radio Shack.

Harlan pressed a button on the side of the radio and spoke. "Yeah, we're ready for you. The sooner, the better."

"Better back up," he added, as he dashed back down the hallway.

I retreated until my back pressed against the far wall of my cell.

The air in the prison hallway glittered and wavered like a heat mirage.

And then, sunlight streamed in like a solid cylinder, as rubble from the edge of a large new hole crumbled down into the hall.

The sunlight was blotted out by something large outside. A deep warbling noise preceded a rope ladder that tumbled down through the hole. A woman in a long, full dress made of a green metallic material descended the ladder, carrying what looked to me like a black leather medical bag. She adjusted a tiny hat of matching material upon her honey blonde hair.

She turned to face Harlan, and the two sized each other up.

"Ma'am," said Harlan, bowing at the waist.

The woman waved her hands. "No time for formal introductions. Are you with us, or with Dixie?"

"I'm with you, Miss Sutton."

I realized with a start that this was Erde Dionne. I called out, "Harlan's with us, despite the uniform, Miss Sutton."

"Actually," said Erde Dionne, taking something the shape and size of a clothes iron out of the bag, "It's Ms. Sutton. I'm married but kept my surname. Please remain away from the bars, and I'll get you out of there in an instant! Mister Harlan, climb up into the ship, if you wish to go with us!"

As I watched, she held the "iron" up to the lock on the bars. With a *zap*, the air around the lock blurred, and the lock was simply *gone.* Dionne favored me with a half-smile and said, "You must be Beta Jules. Pleased to meet you. Let me get your friend out, and we'll be off."

I pushed the cell door out of my way, avoiding the spot where the lock had been, for fear that it might be hot. With another *zap,* Dribbler joined Dionne and me in the hallway. He gave her a salute.

Dionne shooed us toward the ladder. "We really have very little time before my ship is fired on by Dixie, so let us make our escape with all haste!"

I followed Harlan up the ladder, wondering at the colorful flashing lights inside the circular hatchway above us.

I cried out as a familiar face appeared inside that circle. "Hope! You're okay!"

She smiled and beckoned to me. "Climb faster, love. This craft has been damaged before; it would be a shame to let the locals ruin the work Ms. Sutton has done to repair it!"

I emerged into a much larger circular area, with banks of lights and screens surrounding us.

"What, are we on a *spaceship* now?" I asked, my voice quavering with disbelief.

"Not quite," sang Hope. Baby Lucy gurgled and clicked from within a blanket, bundled up and held Hope's arms.

My voice shook as I said, "Hope, Marcy didn't make it through the portal. And they shot Babs and Zamboni."

Hope stared at me, then closed her eyes and seemed to go elsewhere for a moment. When she opened them again, she said, "I believe them to be still alive."

I shook my head. "How can you know that?"

She touched her muzzle with a finger. "They are my kin. I would *know* if they had died. They persist. I am certain we will see them again, though I don't know when."

A man I hadn't noticed yet interrupted. "Not a spaceship, but she can handle the upper stratosphere, at least, if that's where we end up." He wore a slick blue suit of odd design and sat at one of the consoles at the perimeter of the room. But I that's not where we're headed."

I must have stared, because he blinked and said, "Oh, hi there. I'm Lee Green. I'm from Alpha. It's kind of a long story."

Following Dribbler, Dionne joined us and shut the hatch. "He's my husband from another world. The first interdimensional traveler, in fact. At least that we know of, among humans." To Lee, she said, "Darling, it might be wise to make us scarce, one way or another."

A racetrack of lights chased each other around an upper edge of the room, and I had the sensation of motion, but not in any particular direction. The deep warbling sound from earlier accompanied the sense of motion.

The strangest thing happened just then. The sound of rapid gunfire chattered nearby, outside the ship, but rather than impacting the hull, bullets flew *through* the cabin of the ship like the ghosts of angry hornets.

I couldn't help myself, I cried out.

"It's okay," said Lee. "We're out of phase with Erde. Just nudging us a few tenths of a degree askew, into another world. An almost-Erde, if you get my meaning."

"So, wait," said Dribbler, finally joining the conversation. "Are you telling me that this isn't a spaceship, it's a *verseship*? Like Hope's folks fly around in?"

Hope chuckled. "My dear Dribbler, it isn't *like* one of our verseships. It *is* one of our verseships. I'd know this ship anywhere. It's the one my family and friends used to flee Tristel's doom."

Dionne had installed herself at a console next to Lee, and her fingers flew over buttons and screens as she helped fly the ship. "I found the ship, crashed in the Smoky Mountains, on Delta. It's salvage, really," she said, with a subtle lilt in her voice.

"We left it out of phase," sang Hope. "I am surprised you could find her, even in her nonfunctional state. Given your reputation, I am *not* as surprised that you managed to repair her."

I took careful steps, hanging on to occasional railings that were provided, to stand near Erde Dionne. "The Dionne of my world sent us to find you. She said you could help us. And that Hope could help end the Arch Authority. Do you know what she meant?"

Erde Dionne's eyes twinkled as she kept them fixed on the monitors and controls in front of her. "I have a very good idea as to what she meant. Now that we have Hope on board, we might have a chance of rescuing the others."

"Others? You mean the other Tristellians?"

She nodded and gave me a quick glance between keystrokes. "Quite. She can provide a quantum connection between herself and those she traveled with in this ship. All we need now is to find a point outside of spacetime where we may access them, and to be in two places at once!"

"T-two places at once?" I stammered.

She nodded and smiled, and her tiny hat threatened to dislodge itself from her head. "This ship is powered by a type of artificial singularity which allows us to be both in normal space, and outside of it at the same time. We can hardly avoid it. But we need space in a world to anchor, like either end of the Arch gateways. So, the ship is both there, and out in the between space. It is in that between space we may be able to reach Hope's relations. However, she needs to be the conduit to guide them, feet planted firmly upon a world outside, while we guide the others in from between space, using her like a beacon. I am not certain how we can accomplish this. It may take some time to invent a linkage to allow her quantum signature to beckon to the others."

"Hope," I said. "I think I have an idea."

She smiled. "I think I know your idea."

To Dionne, I said, "Hope and I are able to join our minds. While she's outside forming the anchor, I could be here in the ship, acting as this end of the beacon."

Dionne turned her full attention to me, her eyes wide with delight. "That's fantastic! All we need now is a disconnected world in quantum proximity to the Arch worlds, and a vantage in between-space that will serve as a good spot for us to be a beacon and *pull* those Tristellians *through*."

It was my turn to smile again. "I know a great out-of-the-way place we could use. I even have a friend there."

Dionne fixed the angle of the ridiculous little hat on her head, and said, "Wonderful. Except, being disconnected, we'd have to *find* this place you know. Do you have anything *from* there that I could use to get a fix on its location?"

I hooked a thumb in the cable-knit maroon sweater Jimmy'd given me to wear. "Sure do! I'm wearing it! Made on Theta Earth!"

Chapter 25 – Come On In My Kitchen

"Maybe it just won't work for me," I said, brushing a stray bundle of wires out of my face. The helmet on my head weighed more than I'd expected, and the probes in its lining jabbed into my scalp.

"No, no, it'll work, you just have to get tuned in!" said Erde Dionne, twirling dials and nudging slider switches on the console next to me. She frowned at me and tucked a lock of hair behind her ear. "Try to forget where you are. Get into a meditative state."

"Easier said than done," I said, suddenly finding distracting little itches all over my body.

Hope sang, "Perhaps I can help?" Then, she began to hum a tune that sounded familiar, but alien, at the same time.

"Aw, that'll do the trick," said Harlan. "I keep tellin' ya, a recording of this'd sell like hotcakes!"

"Shhh!" hissed Dribbler. "Let them relax."

Hope shifted from humming to singing softly in her own language. Her voice always took on such ethereal beauty in that tongue. I was carried away to the time I had first heard her sing that way. It hit me that it was this very song, which Harlan had explained was a Tristellian lullaby.

My eyes closed, almost of their own volition. My thoughts drifted and wandered; at first, they dwelled on my memories of Hope, such as her singing, and the feeling of being safe within her embrace. And then they wandered. Images of Coral in captivity and of him plunging through the Delta Arch gate in front of me. Of holding baby Lucy on Jimmy's ship.

The cabin of the verseship receded from my senses, and though I could hear people speak, it seemed more like another stream of memories than something going on right now. I heard my name called by several of my friends, and a warmth spread out through my body, from my heart to my fingers and toes.

A cool touch upon my hand brought one voice into focus. Hope sang softly in my ear, "Jules, where are you now?"

Answering her took some sleepy struggle on my part. Like trying to wake from a particularly deep nap, I murmured, "I'm on a boat."

"Very good, Jules. Dionne tells me she wants you to think of the spaces between the worlds. Think of a place where you can see all the Arches at once."

My mind drifted some more, and I watched in passive peace as the colors of the between space washed over the windshield of *La Esperanza* with my memory of Zamboni at the wheel.

And then, my mind flung me out into space, tumbling head over foot, clinging to Dribbler as colorful dots whirled all around us. "I think this is the place. I can feel it."

Something changed. The whirling halted, and I had a different sensation of motion, accompanied by the warbling sound of the verseship's engines.

I murmured, "Hope? What is the name of your verseship?"

Hope's warm affection flowed into me through the touch of her hand. "The ship had another name, but those of us who left in it called her a word in our language that meant 'Exodus'. You could not pronounce it."

"That makes sense. Hope? *Exodus* is moving, isn't she?"

"Yes, love. Dionne is moving her and us through spacetime to match the thoughts in your head."

Someone removed the helmet from my head, and I woke from my reverie as though icy water had been dumped on my head. I let out a yelp and leaped from the chair.

"Oh, sorry!" said Dionne, placing the helmet upon a stand. "I should have given you more warning, but it's vital that we do not drift while I lock in our coordinates."

I had no polite reply to that. Hope squeezed my hand in hers to steady me.

"Now," said Dionne, "let's have that sweater."

Despite being surrounded by friends, I had a sudden attack of shyness. "Well, I—that is—I'm kind of still using it."

Dionne laughed and touched my shoulder with her fingertips. "It's okay. You don't need to take it off. Just pull one of your arms out so I can put the sleeve into the scanner. I don't want your Beta Earth vibes messing up the reading."

The scanner turned out to be a clamshell the size and shape of an adult hand. As she shut the small enclosure on my sleeve, Dionne explained, "I rigged this up to read quantum signatures off of humans, but I've used it to get readings off of inanimate matter plenty of times."

"Got it!" said Lee. "That *is* close to the other Earths. Looks like the name you came up with might just stick, Jules!

Dionne released my sleeve and turned to another console. "Got the coordinates. Okay, this is where things get weird. This ship is about to become a portal between the between spot Jules found, and—what did you call it? Oh! Theta Earth. Try not to think about it too hard, it hurts *my* brain, and I'm used to this sort of thing!"

"It's like Doctor Who, isn't it?" I said.

"What?" said Dionne.

"Never mind, I don't think they have that show on Erde."

"They do on Alpha," said Lee, who winked at me. "And you're not wrong. Except this ship doesn't travel through time, just relative dimensions in space, and it isn't bigger on the inside."

Dribbler and Harlan looked at each other and shrugged.

I laughed. "I guess pop culture references are lost between dimensions."

I think I failed at Dionne's advice; just then I would have sworn I could *feel* myself being stretched between one place and another, as taut as a guitar string. The whole world seemed to vibrate. Or was it just me?

There was also a sensation like being in an elevator. Dionne brought up a screen, which showed a rather familiar bit of real estate.

"That's Lakeshore Drive. Grant Park, even. Why do we keep ending up in Chicago?" I asked. "At least I've got one friend there."

Hope sang, "That is an excellent place for our concert."

"Concert?" said Harlan, Dribbler, and me, all at the same time.

Hope nodded, and handed little Lucy to a surprised Lee. "We will need a great deal of energy to call out to my people across the void. I believe I can draw that from a crowd. Jules, are you up to being a conduit?"

I shook my head. "I have no idea; I've never been one before. What's involved?"

"Take my hand, and we shall link our minds once more. Then, I shall hold an impromptu concert and channel the energy of the crowd through you to broadcast from the ship. Do you trust me, Jules?"

I nodded. "Always, Hope. I'll do my best."

She smiled. "I believe in you. I believe in *us*, Jules." To our new friends, she said, "Mr. Green, Ms. Sutton, do you think you can work out how to pull the others through once we have a connection with them?"

Lee and Dionne looked at each other, shrugged, then turned to nod in unison at Hope. Lee said, "I think we can handle that."

Dionne set us down in Grant Park, and people backed away as we descended, mouths agape.

"What does this ship look like from the outside?" I said.

"You shall soon see," said Hope, offering me her hand.

I took it, and the world doubled around me. Was I looking in Hope's eyes, or was I Hope looking into mine? I'll admit, it was a queasy business once she started moving away and descended through the round hatch.

Harlan protested. "We don't have no gear! No speakers! No amps! No lights!"

"I've got you covered!" said Lee. "Lights are easy. I'll work something out to amplify her."

Dribbler frowned. "I don't have drums. And Babs—"

I hugged him close. "Hope says we'll see her again, Dribs."

He kissed my cheek and said, "If she said so, it must be true. Guess I'll look for a barrel or somethin' to bang."

I smiled up at him. "The show must go on, right?"

He grinned, despite himself, and ruffled my hair. "Yeah. Because Hope says so."

Dribbler descended, and I watched him from both the top and the bottom of the ladder, as Hope stood below. Through her eyes, I saw an incredible sight, and I just had to laugh out loud.

"What is it?" asked Dionne.

I wiped tears from the corners of my eyes. "I can't believe I have to sit out the show where Hope's Tour arrived in a UFO!"

Lee grinned at me. "It's a sweet ride," he agreed.

"Maybe so, but it also makes a hell of a set piece!"

Below, Dribbler addressed the gathering crowd. "People of Chicago! This is Hope! She's on tour, traveling from world to world, sharing music and her namesake with everyone she meets! Please, put your hands together for Hope, the Tristellian!"

With that, he clapped his own hands over his head in a slow beat. Just a few of the Theta Earth Chicagoans joined him. I worried he'd lost the crowd before they'd even begun.

Except then, Hope began to sing. She trilled her voice from the deepest depths of the ocean, warbling up through several octaves to soar up into the sunny skies above Lake Michigan.

The crowd stood entranced as she took them on auditory adventures in her native tongue, even whistling and clicking in time to her song, as though there might be more than one of her standing in front of the fountain.

More people began to clap in time with Dribbler. It spread like a wave outward, and soon hundreds of people clapped in time with the song Hope gave them. And still more filtered in from every direction, growing the crowd's numbers steadily.

All the while, through our link, I had the electrifying sensation of *being* Hope. Her gauzy dress clung to her in the chill November air by the lake. Her body thrilled with excitement as the crowd reacted to her song. Her lungs took in air and forged it into almost tangible sound waves. Her echolocation sense registered every one of the people that gathered around her to listen. She, and I, could feel them all.

And then, Hope slid from the song in her native language to humming a segue to another song. Before she sang a single word, I knew what it would be, even without the link.

Because Hope couldn't pass up a chance to sing the Blues to Chicago. She sang an old song, one from the Delta region, not the Delta dimension. One that had traveled the rails north, from the end of the Mississippi, but not quite to the city of broad shoulders. Hope sang, the opening words an amplified whisper, the opening lines of Robert Johnson's "Come On In My Kitchen", seeming to invite every one of the now thousands of spectators to join her at her kitchen table for a drink.

Dribbler clapped and did something like beatboxing to provide rhythm backing for Hope, and the crowd continued to clap a slow beat along as well.

Maybe it was the familiarity of the song, maybe it was the growing size of the crowd, or maybe their excitement crossed a threshold, but at that moment, a sort of electrical current began to crackle upon Hope's skin. And mine, as well.

To be fair, it had gotten difficult to tell where Hope ended and I began.

The part of me that remained inside the ship said to Dionne, "I can feel it now. We're gathering power. What do I do with it?"

Dionne fussed with some controls and beckoned for me to sit so that she could put the uncomfortable helmet full of probes on my head once more. "Here, you should be able to use this to reach out. Or at least, you should shine like a beacon, if nothing else."

If I'd been confused about being in two places at once before, now I was triply confused, as the between space I'd visualized earlier superimposed itself over the feeling of being Hope singing, the energy crackling upon both our bodies, and the interior of the ship. It was very much like dissociating, since I had to struggle to hang onto my sense of self like a life preserver in choppy waters.

And then, the *other* songs began.

At first, I thought I was hearing the crowd sing along with Hope.

But then, I felt the tug on my awareness of the between space. One of those little dots that weren't stars sang to me. Or rather, something on the other side of one of the dots sang out to me in despair.

"It's working, someone responded," I murmured, from the part of me that sat in the ship with Dionne and Lee.

Lucy gurgled, whistled and clicked, and then she joined in the song as well, humming along since she couldn't form words.

A shock of recognition from the other side ran through me, adding to the electricity crawling all over my skin. In my mind's eye, I reached out a hand toward the dot. Like the portal that led Dribbler and me to Erde, this dot expanded in size as it grew close. An eye peered out at me, then the view widened to show me a Tristellian face. A thought rode along with the distant song: *My child, my baby!*

A mitten-like Tristellian hand grabbed onto mine, and I said, "I have someone! Help me pull them through!"

"Just a moment," said Dionne, working on her console. "Just another adjustment, and—there we go!"

I pulled on the hand and found a damp, wriggling delphine person in my lap and arms.

Dionne helped the newly liberated Tristellian up.

It was then that Lucy spoke her first word. "Mama! Mama-mama-mama!"

Even as the newcomer scooped her baby up in her arms, I felt another tug.

And another. And more.

I pulled one after another of them through, and the interior of the UFO became quite close, with the overwhelming scent of poorly-cared-for Tristellians making my eyes water.

Hope's wordless excitement at our success flowed through me, and outward in the form of her music, drawing cheers of delight from the enthusiastic crowd.

Harlan's voice came to me through Hope's ears. "Uh oh. That can't be good."

With a crack of thunder, Hope turned her head and watched as a vertical line of sudden but persistent lightning widened to form a horizontal oval, its surface shimmering like a trembling sideways pool of mercury.

Someone emerged from the Arch-sized portal.

She wore a navy-blue full length dress, and carried a rifle. She wore my face under that United States of Dixie uniform cap.

And she wasn't alone. A half dozen Dixie soldiers, also armed with long guns, marched in formation out of the portal behind her.

Another rank followed. And another. And another.

They spread out into a long line and leveled their rifle barrels at Hope.

The crowd screamed like a single, terrified organism, as hundreds, thousands of them panicked and ran from the soldiers.

So much happened at once, it's hard to keep it straight in my head which things happened in what order. Let me try to sort it out.

Most immediately, the violence snapped my connection to the between-space. I panicked, thinking we'd leave Tristellians behind, still enslaved by the Arch Authority. Then another Tristellian arrived, wet and disoriented.

"They're doing this without me," I said, amid the confusion.

Dionne nodded and spoke loudly to be heard above the whistles and clicks. "They've firmed up the signal even more. They do this innately, it seems. They're multidimensional in nature."

The room seemed a little less crowded, despite the new arrivals. I glanced at the round hatch in the center of the verseship; Tristellians climbed down the ladder, one after another.

As I said, multiple things happened at once, made more confusing by my awareness being split between the interior of the verseship and what was happening outside around Hope. She saw them emerge and I felt them join her, humming in chorus with her song, standing firm, despite the weapons aimed at them by the U.S. of Dixie soldiers that had arrived through Erde Jules' portal. The humming and singing joined together in a tangible harmony that made my skin prickle with electricity once more.

The thought came from Hope; *Come down and join us, Jules. We need you.*

As I stood, Dionne removed the helmet interface from my head. I meant to tell her my plans, but before I could speak, another thing happened outside.

Another portal, also the size of an Arch gate, appeared on the opposite side of the crowd. An armored vehicle led the charge, followed by a dozen armored ground troops. Among them strode a small figure with short blue hair, wearing a highlighter yellow jumpsuit with an electric blue sash. They wore dark glasses that I realized must be Specs.

The real Delta Jules!

Last out of the Delta gate drove a battered tour bus emblazoned with a stylized Tristellian's face and musical notes, along with the words: Hope's Tour.

La Esperanza had arrived!

I pushed past a couple of Tristellians to make my way to the hatch. As I descended, Jasmine the cat leaped to cling to my back and shoulders. Lee called out to me, "Be careful, Jules! I know better than anyone that meeting yourself is a tricky business! It's always weird, but remember, they're still *you*!"

I didn't have time or mental cycles to consider what his words might mean at the time.

As I touched the ground, my double from Delta called out on a bullhorn, "Soldiers of the United States of Dixie, stand down! You are in violation of the Arch Authority's Code of Conduct. Any harm visited upon the Tristellians will be an act of war, and we will use superior weapons technology to defeat you!"

Lee's words echoed in my mind, and I found I could not imagine a life that led me to take either of my double's position. How could I side with capitalist slavers, or with imperialistic warmongers?

Hope and I shared the briefest of glances. She smiled, filling me with a courage I hadn't known I needed so desperately until that moment. The growing line of Tristellians behind us hummed and whistled and clicked, producing the effect of blues music, if it were produced by a harmonizing acapella orchestra. Believe me, I was there, and I don't think I can explain it any better than that. Whatever you care to call what I heard that day, I felt it with my whole being. Without words, the Tristellian chorus conveyed such lonely sadness and terrible loss that I wept, despite all that went on around me. It was then that I knew just how far we were from the lost world of Tristel, and I ached with the feeling of having no home in the universe to go home to.

Pinned between two small armies, the crowd hunkered down, many with hands over their heads, or shielding others with their bodies. Something swelled in me, and though I mistook it for fear for their safety at first, it blossomed into warm compassion, and a desire to protect them at all costs. And not just them, but I needed to protect the Tristellians we had saved, along with Harlan and Dribbler and Hope. More than that, I needed the troops in either army to be safe.

Out loud, I said to Hope, with certainty that she understood me: "How can we save them all?"

She continued to sing the wordless song with her people, but in my mind, I heard her say, *Not we, Jules. You. Everything has led up to you being the one to save us all. I knew this from the moment we met. Go, speak with the others.*

I looked in the direction of the Dixie portal, and my eyes met with the Jules from Erde. Her expression softened and we nodded at one another. She held up a hand to make the troops from her world stand by, and then she skirted the crowd to walk toward me.

As I turned to look toward Delta Jules, I found them already walking toward me. The Arch troops had aimed their guns at the ground, but they stood tense and ready as well.

Jasmine leaped from my shoulders and trotted out away from Hope and into the open area between her and the crowd, exactly halfway between my two doubles.

Only that lulling, hypnotic Tristellian blues music could be heard as I followed the cat once more into danger and the unknown.

We three Jules from different dimensions met where Jasmine stood, and she weaved around each of our feet in turn. The three of us exchanged long, significant looks.

"You knocked me out, tied me up, and left me in the between space," said Delta Jules to Erde Jules, their voice low and dangerous.

"Your people stranded my father in Arne, left to die at their hands," growled Erde Jules to Delta Jules.

I thought about Lee's words once more, and said, "As much as I hate to say this, deep down, you both know that you would do exactly as the other has done if you were in their place."

Each of them glared at me, and in unison, they said, "I absolutely would *not*!"

And then, the strangest thing happened. We laughed, all three of us, at that moment in the middle of armies. Beneath the Tristellian interdimensional flying saucer with its beautiful singing delphine aliens, and in front of the cowering crowd, it seemed like the world spun around the three of us.

The three of me.

When we stopped laughing, I held out a hand to each of them.

Neither took my hand right away, instead, they shot a look at each other first.

Delta Jules pushed up their Specs to reveal their eyes. Erde Jules' eyes met Delta's across the space between them, and they seemed to come to a mutual decision and each held out both of their hands. We three linked hands, and more than just that touch passed between us. The mental bond I shared with Hope, perhaps powered by the dozen or more Tristellians singing with her, connected me with each of the other Jules. I lost track of whose eyes I looked out of. Erde Jules' corset hugged my ribcage, Delta Jules Specs itched within the hair upon my head.

The memories of two lifetimes flowed into me, mingling with my own. I grew up a daddy's girl to a military father who left and never came back; I'd tried to follow in his footsteps ever since. At the same time, I grew up in fast-paced technological luxury as I climbed the corporate ladder. They learned what it was to drift from job to job, relationship to relationship, never fitting in all that well, seeking something to replace family, but always leaving it behind in the end.

We understood each other on a level beyond intimacy.

We were one.

And yes, I was right. I knew deep down that I would do exactly as each of my interdimensional selves would have done, because they were me, and they had done so.

As one, we thought about the standoff. The Arch Authority needed Tristellians to maintain its worlds-spanning corporate empire. More than that, the Arch worlds had become accustomed to being connected and would feel the loss of those pathways. They needed the Tristellians back to maintain the Arch gates. Meanwhile, the U.S. of Dixie had grievances with their neighbors in Arne and wanted revenge on the Arch Authority for challenging them as a sovereign entity. They wanted to have the freedom of crossing between worlds without Arch interference. They would kill the Tristellians to take power away from the Arch Authority.

My intimate connection with Hope as *family* drove home to the others that Tristellians were *people*, to be loved and cherished, not enslaved or killed. My compassion for the crowd here in Grant Park, Chicago, in Theta Earth spread to the two of them. Violence became unthinkable, despite the needs and wants of the Arch Authority and Erde's United States of Dixie.

Neither could command their army to completely stand down. Neither could solve the underlying problems with a snap of their fingers. Together, we shared the sad despair at the thought of the lives that would be lost if things moved forward as we knew they must.

And then, an idea came to me. "What if the Tristellians shared their verseship technology with us?"

Erde Jules said, "Yeah. And maybe they could be partners, instead of slaves?"

Delta Jules smiled. "Maybe all worlds could be empowered to create other means to travel from one to another?"

"What we need now," I said, "is to make everyone understand this as we do."

Hope's thoughts came to me just then. *Would you say that you could use some hope?*

I laughed with the other two of me and we agreed that would be perfect. I sent the thought to Hope and both of the other Jules: *I know just the song.*

Hope nodded to Dribbler, who began to clap once more.

Dribbler called out to the crowd, "We could all use some hope right now. Rock and roll gonna save your soul!"

And then, the chorus of Tristellians sang out the opening words to Journey's "Don't Stop Believin'".

A wave of music and emotion broke upon the crowd and everyone stood up to cheer and clap along with Dribbler.

I could almost see the wave flow out to overwhelm both armies and cover the interdimensional portals.

As the song went on, the crowd joined in. And then, the soldiers put down their weapons and began to clap and sing along.

I know no one believes this part when I tell the story. I know that those back home in Erde, and Delta, and the other Arch worlds don't fully understand. But at that moment, during that song, each and every one of us understood each other as one.

More than just the three of us being one, *all* of us were one. We knew that we always had been, and always would be. The song that Hope and her kin sang transcended the words of the pop song that reached our ears by reaching into our very essences as sentient beings, and we all knew that if we had lived the lives of any of the others of us, we would have followed the same path and made the same decisions.

That compassion I'd felt for the crowd spread to each and every person there, and from that day on, we were changed forever, having seen through the eyes of hundreds of others while feeling their pain and joys and unique outlook on life as though we always had and always would.

The message of Hope's music was in her name, but it was something we all found within each other that day.

And then the song ended.

Everyone stood, stunned, for a full minute, staring at one another with new eyes and changed souls.

And then, even though the connection had ended, we all cheered and clapped as one.

The rest of the concert was a blur. I know that I hugged each of my other selves, and we ran to greet Marcy and a bandaged Babs as they burst out of *La Esperanza*. We shook hands with soldiers and spectators. We sang along with Tristellians, and we shouted out requests that Hope was happy to fulfill.

It was the best party I'd ever been to.

At the end of the concert, there at the end of the tour, Hope called out to everyone present to say, "My friends, this is the end but also the beginning! Don't stop believing! Let us hold each other close, even when we leave this place. Thank you for being you, I love you one and all!"

Arms encircled me, and the scent of Dribbler's sweat let me know who it was that held me.

Before I could say anything to him, another set of arms wrapped around us, and Hope's body pressed against me. She murmured in my ear, "Jules, you were fantastic!"

Soon enough, our group hug broke up, as Marcy and Babs cut in to embrace each of us individually. Harlan stood awkwardly nearby, but Hope pulled him into the circle to share the love and triumph. Jasmine headbutted our legs, not to be denied her share of adoration.

"So, what happens now?" asked Dribbler.

Harlan looked over his shoulder at the Erde gate and its celebrating soldiers. "Guess we all go home and work out this new way of getting around from world to world."

"Home," breathed Dribbler. "I just can't go back to Gamma."

Marcy and Babs shook their heads, agreeing with Dribbler, their fingers intertwined.

Hope gazed downward. She sang, "You know I have no home to return to. But I hear my kin are negotiating an expedition back in the direction of Tristel. Perhaps we will find a world alike enough to that place to begin again. What about you, Jules?"

I smiled, but sighed, my heart heavy all of a sudden. "I could go back and try to make it work with Sam, but she's already moved on. Guess I could just go back to Beta and maybe see if my world's Dionne needs help saving the world. She might overlook my spotty resume in light of recent events, don't you think?"

"You could," sang Hope, touching the wetness of my cheek. "But it would seem to be a waste of your talents."

"My talents?" I said. "I've never stuck with any one thing long enough to get very good at it. What do you have in mind?"

She smiled and pulled me closer. "I only just hired you onto my crew, it would be a shame to see you go!"

I pushed her away to look her in the eyes. "Don't tease. Don't you dare. You just said you were going off to find a new home with your kin. It's hard enough saying goodbye to the most wonderful person I've ever met, without being taunted about it."

"Jules," she sang, her smile softening. "Have you learned nothing about me? What do I always say?"

As one, the crew shouted, "The show *must* go on!"

I looked from one face to another, certain that I must have missed a meeting somehow. "But how?"

Hope cradled my face in her smooth hands and kissed me. When she drew back, she said, "I was thinking. It's going to take a while for the local worlds to sort out all the details. Only then can my people go searching for a new home. So, in the meantime, what do you think about a spectacular farewell tour?"

I took a step back from Hope to look around at my friends. Jasmine leaped into my arms and I petted her head. "You know I'm in! But Hope, what about your kin?"

Hope held her arms wide, taking in all of us there. "My people value family above all else. We travel in pods, like the dolphins of your world, each of us taking care of the others. You, my crew, are all my family. My pod. Let's get things settled, then we can hit the road once more!"

"How will we get from world to world, while they work things out?" asked Dribbler.

"I had a little talk with Erde Dionne, back on the ship. She thinks it would be child's play for her to rig a bigger version of the portal gun as a permanent part of *La Esperanza*. We could go anywhere we pleased, like a little road-bound verseship. Who's with me?"

Dribbler raised his hand, a goofy grin upon his face.

Babs and Marcy raised their joined hands together, giggling.

Even Harlan raised his hand, an odd look of wonder glinting in his eyes.

Sitting upon my shoulder, Jasmine raised a paw and let out a long, heartfelt meow.

All eyes fell upon me.

"Well, Jules?" said Marcy. "Are you ready to run away with us?"

I raised my hand, glancing at Jasmine. "Why not? I could do a lot worse than to follow a cat into the unknown. Again."

About the Author

E. Chris Garrison writes fantasy and science fiction novels and short stories.

Her urban fantasies feature ghosts, demonic possession, and sinister fairy folk delivered with a "lightly dark" side of humor.

Chrissy's Trans-Continental series is a steampunk adventure with a transgender woman protagonist. The series is set in one of the worlds in Chris's dimension-hopping science fiction adventure, Reality Check, also published by Silly Hat Books. Silly Hat Books released Alien Beer and Other Stories, a collection of her short stories, in 2017. Chrissy's latest release, in early 2021 was Trans Witch: College of Secrets, which has been her most popular book to date.

Chrissy lives in Indianapolis, Indiana, with her wife and their many cats. She also enjoys gaming, home brewing beer, and finding innovative uses for duct tape. Keep up on the latest news and releases from Chrissy at:

https://sillyhatbooks.com/

Photo Credit: (c) Ellie Sophia Photography
www.elliesophia.com